Where the Heart is

JASINDA WILDER

ROM
Wilder

Where the Heart is

Prologue

Six years ago I conceived my beautiful, gorgeous, fabulous little boy, Alex. I'm kind of ashamed to admit it, but the date still stands as the hottest day of my life, and one I do not regret even slightly, despite the fact the man in question turned out to be a rat bastard and every kind of piece of shit. Since then my life has been all messed up and screwed over and irredeemably fucked except for two factors: Alex was born, and his conception entailed some seriously hot sex.

I never saw Tom again after that—unless you count the time I saw him for less than five minutes. I was six months pregnant and had spent the preceding six months hunting his ass down to inform him of our little "oops." Or, more correctly, *his* oops; he'd assured me he was "fixed."

I was thirty-two at the time and managing a restaurant . . . okay, well, fine, managing a titty bar. *Managing*, mind you, not dancing, or waitressing. I'd done my time waitressing in New York, then LA, and then Nashville, and then Chicago, in my pursuit of a career as a musician. Which had gone belly up . . . or, rather, never really got off the ground.

I was told over and over and over again that I had talent, I had the looks, and I had the stage presence, but the timing just wasn't right, or my songs sounded like a major artist's . . . only better. It all just meant that the years got whittled away little by little, and suddenly I was thirty-two with a few songs I'd written playing on the radio, performed by another artist, for which I was paid a laughable amount. The result was the only real work experience I had was waitressing, and I was going nowhere with that career, so when I was offered a job managing a strip bar, I took it because it meant a steady paycheck, and I wouldn't have to rely on tips to make a living.

And then I'd met Tom at the gym, and we slept together a few times, and then a few more, and then we met at his hotel room downtown and had a magical afternoon . . . and I ended up pregnant.

Guess what the strip bar didn't offer? Health insurance.

Guess who hadn't ever bothered to get Medicaid

because I was never sick, and thus never needed it? Me.

I found out the hard way you can't get pregnancy coverage *after* you're already pregnant? True.

So guess who ended up stuck with a massive hospital bill?

And guess which strip bar didn't take kindly to me needing a few weeks off after having a baby?

There went that job.

Anyway, about six months into the pregnancy, when I was really starting to show, I finally tracked down Tom's address—and let me tell you, that fucker did *not* want to be found. I showed up, unannounced at his door, at two in the morning. He lived in the nice, upper-crust end of suburban Chicago. A brick house, huge and beautiful. Manicured lawn. Four-car garage. Porsche in the driveway.

I pounded on the door until he answered. He was naked as he flung the door open. Just as hung and ripped as ever . . . and *not* pleased to see me.

He stared at me, as if absorbing my presence, and then his gaze slid down to my rounded belly.

"Oh, hell no," he'd snarled.

"Oh, hell *yes*," I'd snarled back. "And yes, I *know* it's yours."

He'd stared at me again, and then held up a finger in a *wait a minute* gesture. He disappeared then reappeared a few minutes later with a check in his hand worth ten grand.

And I noticed a ring on his ring finger, which had never been there before, nor had there been a tan line, which meant he must take it off a lot.

I stood there staring at his check, and his cock, and his house, and the marble floor, and the chandelier over his head, when a young woman several years my junior descended the stairs, wrapped in a thin robe that highlighted her perfectly fake tits, and her perfectly fake tan, and her perfectly fake blonde hair.

She'd sidled up behind him, leaned against his back, stroking his chest and stomach, as if trying to tease me. "Really, Tom? Another one? Pay her and come back to bed. I want you again."

I waved the check at them. "He did pay me. But I'm not sure it's enough."

The woman—Tom's trophy wife, I assumed—snatched the check out of my hand, glanced at it, sniffed, and tore it up. She reappeared after a moment with another check, this one for twenty-five thousand. "There. Now leave, and don't come back. He's a lawyer, and our lawyers have lawyers, so don't think about trying anything."

"He does this a lot, then?" I'd asked. "Knocks up girls and then pays them off to vanish?"

She'd eyed me up and down. "I'm not sure you count as a *girl*, honey. A little past your prime for that."

Damn. That had hurt. The only retort I could manage was, "You know, if I'd known all along it was like this, I'd have tried to get some goodies out of you."

"You were a side-fuck, Delta, not a sugar-baby," Tom replied.

He was wearing a watch, something gold and glittering with diamond insets. He stripped it off and tossed it at me, careless of whether I caught it or not. "Here. Now, seriously, get the fuck out of here." I took the money and the Rolex, and I got the fuck out.

I still own that Rolex, although there have been times when I needed money and it was the only asset I had. But I kept it because I want a reminder of my bad decisions and how I got to where I am today. It's way too big, but if I wear it with a sexy little black dress, I can pass for someone I'm not. Which is useful when you're a single mother trying to get laid.

J onny Núñez gives me the tingles, and I have never before had the tingles.

I'm on the beach sitting next to him, and we are both exhausted, mentally and physically.

He's worked non-stop since I first showed up in Ft. Lauderdale two days ago. And he says he was here for three days before that. I have yet to see him sleep for more than a couple of hours at a time, and when he does sleep he lies down wherever he is, pillows his head on his arm, and dozes off immediately. When he wakes up he is alert and energetic, working tirelessly and methodically, helping the first responders attempt to find survivors in the hell that is what is left of Ft. Lauderdale after a Category 5 hurricane blew through. He seems to be inexhaustible. He does the work of three men and makes it look easy.

Curiously, we both arrived in Ft. Lauderdale for the same reason—to find my sister, Ava. By some miracle she is alive. She took cover in her bathtub when the storm first hit and that action, along with a bottle of water, saved her life. It took three days to find her, and Jonny was one of the first on scene.

Ava is in the hospital, crowded into a room with three others. She's dehydrated, exhausted, and suffering from shock; she has a concussion, despite not remembering hitting her head at any point. Given how crowded the hospital rooms and hallways are, there's no way for us to be with her except for occasional visits, and there's so much work to be done. So we work.

We've taken a break to have coffee and sandwiches, and I'm so tired I can hardly eat. I'd love to fall asleep, but I'm overtired, so I just sit and let my mind drift.

My head is resting on Jonny's shoulder. I'm not trying to be cute or coy, I'm completely flattened by exhaustion. He doesn't seem to mind. He hasn't said anything, so I'm assuming he's okay with it. If there is one thing I've learned about Jonny in the past couple of days, it's that he is a man of few words.

From his actions alone I can tell he's salt of the earth. Strong. Solid. Fit. Handsome, but not flashily so. Exotic. Ruggedly sexy. Deep-set dark eyes narrowed in a permanent squint. Weathered and darkly tanned, his Latino skin is scarred in places, and he seems to favor one of his legs. Black hair, thick and wavy and messy, dirty and unwashed at the moment, is flecked with debris and mud and who knows what else, finger-combed straight back, curling around his collar. He has scruff on his jaw, almost but not quite a beard, and he has a scar on his jawline going from right cheekbone through his beard to his chin. His voice is smooth, with a musical Hispanic lilting, rolling accent.

I made the decision to stick with Jonny, help with the cleanup, and look for survivors and bodies, but I hardly know why. I should try to spend more time with Ava, or I should get back to St. Pete's and be with Alex.

I check with my mom and dad every day to let them know how Ava is doing, and to hear how things are going with Alex. He sounds like he's having the time of his life with Gramma and Grampa, as he calls them. Eating sweets and junk food and watching movies all day, probably being spoiled rotten. But God knows he deserves a little spoiling, since I have trouble keeping a roof over our head and food in the fridge.

For six years I've kept the money Tom gave me as a nest egg, a cushion. I try not to rely on it, or use it unless I have to. It'll go quick, if I'm not careful. I work all the hours I can, provide for Alex on my own, and pretend as if that money isn't in the bank. My neighbor, Mrs. Allen, is a retired widow, and she picks up Alex from the school bus each day and watches him till I get home. Even working double shifts most days, it's all I can do to pay rent, utilities, and buy food. I have an apartment in a decent neighborhood. It wouldn't be as tight if I lived in a less desirable area, but I want him to grow up safe. I want him to go to a nice school. Get a decent education and grow up to be a successful adult. Which means I work my ass off to afford a nicer apartment in a nicer area than I really can afford, but he doesn't know that, and he never will.

Ava always said I was easily distracted, and prone to oversharing. Which, I suppose is true. It's why I sucked at school and never even tried to go to college. I focused on music, writing songs, and honing my acoustic guitar skills, booking gigs at coffee shops and dive bars. For a while, in my twenties, I actually made a decent living on music alone. But my music career wasn't going anywhere, and I had to have a day job to support the gigging. Which meant I gigged less and less, and then, eventually, not at all.

And it's been six years since I last gigged.

I still play though. When I get home from work at three or four in the morning, Alex is asleep and I'm too wired from work to sleep; I get out my battered and beloved Yamaha, tune her up, and I play quietly and sing my favorite songs. I even write some new ones, since I can't seem to help it. My songs are usually bitter Ani DiFranco-esque pieces about how men are assholes, and quasi-artistic pieces about how life is hard, told via metaphor.

Tingles, tingles. My mind drifts back to the present, and I am acutely aware of how I feel sitting next to Jonny.

My ear and cheek tingle where they rest against Jonny's shoulder.

My hip, where it touches his, tingles.

He lifts a hand to munch on his sandwich, and then lowers it, and his forearm touches mine, and my skin tingles.

Why am I tingling?

It's stupid. I shouldn't tingle. I never tingle.

I mean, after a really nice orgasm, I'll tingle for a few seconds, but it goes away. Just innocently making contact with someone has never made me tingle before.

I know nothing about him. Nothing. NOT A DAMN THING. He doesn't talk much, if at all. He just works tirelessly, like a machine.

He listens to me when we take breaks together. I'm the original Chatty Cathy my dad used to say, and I do enough talking for both Jonny and me. He watches me with those intense, inscrutable dark eyes of his, nods and asks probing questions, and never seems surprised by my tendency to blab what other people might consider personal info, or TMI—I'm a constant fountain of TMI.

He seems utterly without judgment. He accepts me and listens to me. And I don't get the sense that he's only tolerating me or keeping his judgment to himself.

I LIKE HIM.

Dammit.

That means he'll probably turn out to be an asshole.

If I'm honest, I have to admit I'm preoccupying myself with Jonny and the cleanup efforts in an attempt to not freak out about—well, everything.

I'm thinking about Ava, and the hurricane, and her husband Chris. Ava hasn't heard from Christian for a long time—the last time they spoke he was out at sea somewhere off the coast of Africa. I'm also worrying about how many days of work I'm missing and that when I return to Chicago I'll probably have to find a new job. I miss my Alex, and I'm worried that he'll like living with Gramma and Grampa more than with me and I'll end up alone.

And, oh yeah, Jonny. I've been thinking a lot about him.

And liking him.

And reminding myself about the mantra I've had looping through my head since I met him:

Don't sleep with Jonny.
Don't sleep with Jonny.
Don't sleep with Jonny.

I'm putting the reminder on repeat in my head, because I have to at least try to be a good girl.

But I'm not. I'm a bad girl.

I like sex, and I'm reckless and impulsive, and I'm a terrible judge of people—the exact opposite of Ava, in other words. She's perfect and always has been. She excelled in school and never got in trouble. A good writer. Sweet. Funny. Classy. Effortlessly elegant. Effortlessly skinny. She snagged Christian without even trying, and he turned out to be a mega-popular novelist with books being turned into movies, and he makes a shitload of money. Now Ava drives a fucking *Mercedes-Benz* and I'm . . . just me, still struggling like I've always struggled.

I am the exact opposite of Ava. I was bad at school. I was always in trouble, because I was always hanging out with the wrong crowd. And I'm dyslexic, or dysmorphic or something, or just not book smart, and I can't write or read very well.

I'm sarcastic and sassy and rude, and I talk too much and spout too much highly personal information without thinking about it. I'm not classy or elegant at all, and I have to work out like a fiend to keep my ass from ballooning into something with its own zip code. I hate running. I drive a fourteen-year-old Accord. I have no boyfriend, much less a wealthy and successful and admittedly gorgeous husband like Christian St. Pierre.

What I have going for me: a beautiful voice, talent with a guitar, a knack for song writing, and a cool name. I mean, come on, Delta Martin says music star, doesn't it? I've always thought so, but the music industry didn't seem to agree.

I also have naturally big and still-perky-at-thirty-eight-despite-having-breastfed tits. That's pretty much it as far as my positive qualities go.

I'm good at sex, so I've got that going for me, too, I suppose. I give a hell of a BJ, I'm flexible enough to get into some really neat positions . . . and I have the libido of a girl twenty years my junior.

Which, currently, is a problem.

As I said, I'm trying to remind myself that I should NOT, under any circumstances, allow myself to sleep with Jonny Núñez, because it's bad timing, it can't go anywhere, and he's probably an asshole or transient or both. Plus, I have enough on my plate to deal with; I'm a thirty-eight-year-old single mom and nobody wants to be saddled with that baggage, and I'm at the stage of my life where I'm prone to getting clingy and, now I have to be here for Ava, because God knows she's gonna need a hell of a lot of help between the storm and Christian going missing.

So, to repeat: sleeping with Jonny is a *bad* idea.

God, I'm *so* gonna sleep with Jonny, and I know I'm going to regret it.

Don't sleep with Jonny.
Don't sleep with Jonny.
Don't sleep with Jonny.

"I'll make sure to keep my hands to myself, since you feel so strong about it." His voice is a low rumble, amused.

What?

Oh no.

"Did I . . . Was I talking out loud?" I ask, straightening up off his shoulder.

He rumbles again, and it's a laugh, I think. "Yeah, you were chanting it. Been whispering 'don't sleep with Jonny' for, like, five minutes now."

"Shit. My mouth sometimes runs away from my brain."

"Funny. I got the exact opposite problem."

"I've noticed."

"Jonny, listen, I just—"

He gazes at me, and his eyes are totally opaque and unreadable. "Why shouldn't you sleep with Jonny? Just asking for a friend."

For once my mouth is shut, instead of blabbing all the reasons I've been obsessively going over in my head.

I blurt out, "I, um. Because I want to."

"That's not a reason not to sleep with Jonny. Sleeping with Jonny is a good thing, from what I hear. And if you want to, then . . . presto, not a problem."

I laugh. "But it's a bad plan. For me and for you."

"I'm not hearing too much by way of actual reasons."

"There are a lot of them, but they'd just bore you."

"I don't get bored very easy. Try me."

"Um. All this, to start with?" I wave around us.

He shrugs. "Good enough reason for now, I guess. Later, though, it may not stick."

"My sister, Ava, for one," I say. "And . . . Christian, for another—her husband, my brother-in-law and your best friend. Which kind of connects us in a weird way."

He frowns. "Gotta give you that one. Those are both good reasons."

I sigh. "And because I have a son." I sigh again, more heavily, because this is when dudes tend to check out on me.

"What's his name?"

I'm silent for a moment, because this isn't how this conversation usually goes, leaving me at a loss. "Um. His name is Alex."

"How old is he?"

People don't usually ask his name, much less how old he is. Well, okay, that's not completely true. Little old ladies, grandmas and grandpas, cashiers, servers, cops, security guards, etc., they all ask his name, because he's a ridiculously adorable little human being. But guys who want to get me naked? They don't ask his name.

So either Jonny isn't like other guys, or he doesn't want to get me naked.

Not sure which; he's a hard man to read.

I also don't want to read anything into this and create things that aren't there . . .

Like feelings.

And potential.

And the fact that Jonny might not be an asshole like every other male on the planet.

I have an absurd desire to light a bonfire on this beach, play my guitar, and sing.

If there was a bonfire, and a guitar, I would.

I really want Jonny to know I'm, like, a person with something to contribute to the world, besides a skill with a pen and an order pad, and my banging-for-any-age-let-alone-a-thirty-eight-year-old body.

I want him to . . .

I want him to *like* me, for who I am as a person.

I haven't wanted anyone to like me since my senior year of high school when I had a crush on the starting quarterback of the FSU varsity football team.

I *want* Jonny to like me.

Which creates a question and thus a conundrum: if I want *him* to like me, then I'm pretty sure I have to like myself first. That's how it works, I'm pretty sure.

And at this stage in my life, I'm not positive I like myself very much.

Which is a problem.

Or not, if I keep to my determination that I'M NOT GOING TO SLEEP WITH JONNY NÚÑEZ.

If I don't sleep with him, it won't matter if I like him, or if he likes me, or if I like myself.

Although . . .

I could *JUST* sleep with him, in which case it wouldn't matter whether he likes me, or I like me.

Just sleeping with him isn't really a possibility, though. I'm gonna be clingy, and I'm going to like him, and I'm going to be a problem for both of us.

Dammit.

This was supposed to be a visit to my sister, to help her through a difficult, emotional time in her life.

It wasn't supposed to create a crisis for me.

God, I'm so gonna sleep with Jonny.

2

Dawn breaks slowly in front of us, a low glimmer of pink staining the rippling marble slab that is the sea.

I'm deeply, intensely uncomfortable right now: Delta fell asleep with her head on my shoulder, and so I'm sitting on the beach, my back against the retaining wall separating the beach from the boardwalk. I slid her down so her head was resting on my lap, which is where she is now, right on top of my screaming bladder. My legs are numb. I only managed to doze a little, seeing as I was sitting up, but I didn't want to disturb her, and I still want to let her sleep as long as she can.

It's truly bizarre, this situation.

I've known Delta for about seventy-two hours now, and the frenetic, driving pace of the rescue efforts thrust us into an unnaturally close bond. I've spent literally every moment of the last three days with Delta Martin, who was, until the tin boat dropped her off, a complete stranger. Now . . . it's hard to remember what life was like before she showed up. That may be exhaustion speaking, of course, but she's wormed her way into my head.

Normally, if a girl were to fall asleep on my shoulder on the beach, I'd slip out from under her and be on my way. But with Delta, I don't think she'd think anything of it if I were to do so, slip out, hit the port-a-potty, and go back to digging out survivors and the deceased.

But for some reason, I don't.

I stay put.

My bladder screams and aches, my back hurts from being in one position for so long, and I'm so exhausted I'm literally delirious. Yet something about Delta pins me in place. Not her, in a literal, physical sense, since she's light as a feather, but something less tangible.

Something about the way she has her face on my thigh, her mouth slightly open, soft, feminine breaths sighing out, her hair a messy tangle across her face in inky-black strands. Something about the way she's curled on her side, knees drawn up. Something about her vulnerability.

Something about the way she's worked, the last few days, even after Ava was rescued. She never questioned it, just kept right on going beside me. We have taken a break, once per day, to go see Ava. I go with her, escorting her to the hospital and through the crowded halls, and I wait quietly while Ava and Delta murmur to each other in low tones, and then I escort her back.

Ava, while I'm there, avoids even looking at me.

I think she's terrified of what I have to say about Christian. I understand that, and I'm willing to wait until she's ready. I mean, as far as I know, all Ava really knows about me is that Christian is my friend and sailing partner, that we've known each other for several years, and that we're pretty close. Which must be nervewracking, to her, to know I have the last item he ever touched, and that he gave it to me to give to her? What does that say? I can only imagine how that must feel to her.

I have the box, tucked away beside me. I've claimed this little spot on the beach as mine, leaving the box and a small collection of supplies I've stockpiled—bottles of water, an unopened bottle of rum I found floating down the street, a dirty and tattered blanket rescued from the rubble, and a dented and rusty but useable flashlight.

Honestly, living on the beach on burnt coffee and stale, flat sandwiches, my only belongings rescued from rubble, is a throwback to my teenage years. Living in tent cities, wandering from slum to slum, city to city, barely surviving, eating literal trash sometimes, everything I owned in a backpack, and those belongings were all dumpster-diving prizes. Not the most amazing memories to be reliving, truth be told, but it is what it is.

I've been homeless since I was thirteen. I haven't had

a permanent home—at least one that didn't float—since then. My homes have been berths on boats, a hotel or motel or hostel occasionally, often the beach, and sometimes a woman's bed for a week or two. That's my life, my identity: I belong nowhere, to no one; home is wherever I lay my head; the world is my home.

This is different, though. Why, I'm not sure.

The fact is: Chris is gone, possibly dead, and I have no way of knowing for sure. I'm responsible for telling his wife, who won't even look at me, so far.

And Delta.

She makes this different, too, in a distinctly intangible way.

She stirs, murmuring unintelligibly. Wiggles, brings her hand up to her face, rubs her nose, and then wiggles again, seeking a more comfortable position as she sleeps. In the process of seeking a new position, her hand rests near her face, palm down . . . directly on my cock.

She's asleep, I remind myself. It's not intentional. My body doesn't seem to want to listen, though. All my body knows is that a hand that's not mine is resting on—and almost clutching—my cock.

Which is responding according to nature.

I focus on breathing, staring at the sea and the sunrise turning the pink stain into a golden-crimson-peach glow on the horizon. I focus on having to piss, on the gulls hopping along the sand and wheeling overhead, keening occasionally. I focus on anything and everything except Delta, and the accidental, meaningless, totally co-incidental positioning of her hand.

It doesn't work.

I no longer have to pee, because I'm hard as a rock, and there's not a damn thing I can do about it.

I try to will it to go away, but it won't.

I think of my mother, my sisters, of the hurricane that took Chris and *The Hemingway*, of nuns and puppies and stray cats and rats scurrying in the gutters . . .

I'm nearly successful at getting the hard-on to go away . . . it's starting to subside a little, slowly and gradually.

But then Delta stirs again, makes a muzzy, sleepy sigh, and her head digs into my thigh, and her hand tightens. Squeezes. Flexes, releases, and squeezes again.

Intentionally.

As if she's waking up but hasn't opened her eyes yet and is attempting to discern exactly what it is she's feeling.

I know the moment she truly wakes up, and the next moment, when she realizes . . . well, the rest of the situation.

Her eyes flutter, and her vivid ultramarine eyes flit from mine, to her hand, and back up to my eyes. She blinks and doesn't remove her hand.

I do not blink, do not breathe. I remain utterly still, unsure now what this moment is, and what I'm supposed to do next.

Her hand squeezes again as her eyes remained fixed on mine. And then, with a deliberateness that leaves nothing to question, she traces the outline of my erection behind my shorts, from top to bottom, and ends up grasping me, her eyes on mine.

"Delta," I murmur, and then I don't know what else to say.

She blinks up at me. "Hi, Jonny." A small, shy smile curves her lips.

I shift in the sand, flex my back, my buttocks, my shoulders, willing Delta to let go of me before I run the risk of indulging in curiosity. Which, as she said, is a bad idea for both of us. This situation is untenable, and the bond we feel is false, created by the closeness and the constant contact, and the intensity of the high-octane emotions that comes with digging out corpses and wounded survivors. It's not real, this weird, intense, erotic moment.

I remember her chant from last night/early this morning—*don't sleep with Jonny, don't sleep with Jonny, don't sleep with Jonny*—and I know she's right to remind herself of that. Yeah, she's attractive. Yeah, she may feel some stirrings of desire for me, as I do for her. But there are no real emotions in this. And if there were? What then? I'm a nomad, and I owe it to Chris to be there for his wife however I can, which, obviously, doesn't include sleeping with her sister out of some misplaced chemistry born through a dramatic situation.

But Delta isn't letting go. Nor is she looking away from my eyes. Nor is she making any move to alter this moment. If anything, she adjusts her grip on me to more fully and intimately cup me.

I let out a breath, wondering how the hell I'm going to navigate this. "You, um . . . fell asleep." I hunt for something else to say. "Didn't want to disturb you."

She smiles up at me. "So you've been sitting here all night, letting me sleep?"

I shrug. "Yeah, sure. I can sleep anywhere."

"That was very nice of you, Jonny." Her smile shifts, and her gaze breaks mine, flits to her hand. "I feel like I should thank you. I slept better than I have in days."

"Not a big deal."

Her grip tightens. "I mean, Jonny, I should *thank* you."

I stare down at her. Try to be a more virtuous man than I usually am. "Don't need to. All I did was let you sleep a few hours."

"You must have been uncomfortable, though."

"Eh, not so bad." That's a lie: my back and butt are a mess of knots.

She slides her hand up and then down, tracing my erection with her touch. "You're kind of hard to read, but for some reason I feel like that's a lie."

I force myself to stillness. "Maybe a little. It's not a big deal."

"Well, still, thank you." She eyes her hand, and the

thick bulge under it. "I'm . . . *very* grateful."

I'm an honest man. I don't play head games, I don't worry about being polite, or tactful. I say and do whatever seems right and true and natural. In this moment, though, I don't know what is right or true or natural. Part of me wants to let her thank me. I mean, her hand *does* feel good, and she *is* a gorgeous woman—I'm a man, and any excuse to be touched like this is hard to refuse. But then, she's Christian's sister-in-law. Christian is missing. Ava is in the hospital. Ft. Lauderdale is in ruins, hundreds if not thousands are dead, there are millions of dollars in damage, survivors to rescue, dead to bury. It's not my city, not my home, but it's in my nature to help, to pitch in with a will when someone is in need. It's just how I am. And this is the utterly most inappropriate time for any kind of indulgence in desire.

I catch at her wrist, halting her movement. "Don't need to thank me, Delta."

Her eyes reflect confusion and disappointment. "No? What if I want to?"

"Those are different things, doing something to thank me, and doing it because you want to."

"True. Ends up the same, though, for both of us." She squeezes, and short of physically removing her hand from me, I can't stop that, and dammit, but I don't want to. "Doesn't it?"

I make a sound that's a cross between a growl and a hiss. "Not necessarily."

The corners of her mouth tip up, amused and aroused, and her eyes betray the humor she finds in my discomfort. "No?"

I shake my head. "You do somethin' like this because you feel like you should thank me, then it's . . ." I shrug, a roll of one shoulder. "It'd feel kind of like a transaction, to me. You doin' somethin' out of . . . obligation."

Her smile becomes even more amused. "That's not what I meant."

"Sounded like it to me, though." I hold her wrist, but she's still squeezing me, a gentle throb of pressure that's definitely getting to me, and I fight to hold the thread of why I'm not supposed to let this happen. "You doing something like what you seem to be inclined to do because it's what you *want* to do . . . now *that* might be a different story."

"I like the sound of that story," Delta says. "I just meant the whole thank you thing as . . ." She laughs, a bright, amused, self-aware, slightly embarrassed sound. "I was being coy, Jonny, that's all."

"Ain't into coy, Delta."

"What *are* you into, then, Jonny?"

We're saying each other's names a lot, for some reason, and she still has her head resting on my thigh, which is a lot more intimate now that she's awake than it was when she was asleep. She's still squeezing my cock, applying pressure gently, rhythmically, insistently, and it's maddening and arousing at the same time.

"Saying things like they are."

"That happens to be my speciality. I can't really help saying things like they are. Drives most people crazy." She shifts, and her face is a few inches closer to my torso and her hand. A simple shift in position, but it's laced with promise, and I'm having a hell of a time ignoring that unspoken promise.

"That so?" I swallow hard and have to remember to breathe and to keep still and to leave my hands where they are, one on her wrist and one in the sand beside my hips. "You? Drive people crazy? Nah." I smile, so she knows I'm teasing her.

"Right? What a wild thought, that I would drive anyone crazy." She bites her lower lip, tugging at the corner with her upper teeth, and then her tongue peeks out and slides along that plump lower lip, and it's not my face she's eyeing as she does this.

"You being coy again, Delta?"

She shakes her head. "Me? Never."

"Then what exactly is going on here?" I tighten my grip on her wrist in indication of my meaning.

A shrug of a lithe shoulder. "I don't know." She bites that lip again, which shouldn't make my heart thump, but it does. "I just woke up like this."

"I think this situation has kind of gotten away from us, Delta."

She nods. "Out of hand, you might say."

"Well, no. If anything, it's well *in* hand."

She snorts softly. "Now who's being coy?"

I laugh wryly. "Just making a joke."

The humor bleeds out of Delta's eyes as she tests my grip on her wrist. "Am I making you uncomfortable, Jonny? For real."

"I'm just . . ." I shrug. "You said it last night, this isn't really the best time for . . ." I squeeze her wrist and then let go. "This kind of thing."

"I know what I said last night."

I rest my hand on her shoulder. "But?"

"But . . . that was before I woke up with my hand on your dick, Jonny."

"I didn't put it there," I say, maybe a little too quickly and insistently. "You moved, and your hand landed there, and I didn't want to wake you up. And . . . well, some things are an automatic instinct. You woke up before I could figure out what the right thing to do was."

She smiles. "You getting hard was nothing but an instinctive reaction, huh?"

"I . . . um. Well, yeah. I mean, a beautiful woman has her head on my lap, and then she puts her hand on my dick, yeah, it's instinct to get hard."

"A beautiful woman, huh?" She rolls her eyes at me. "Don't oversell it, buddy."

"Not an oversell. An undersell, if anything."

"I was hot as hell twenty years ago. I was beautiful ten years ago. Now? I'm striking at best."

I stare her down. "Not how I see it." I let my hand

rest on the back of hers, and our fingers tangle, mine sliding between hers. "And that has nothing to do with where your hand is. Just my honest opinion."

"Just your honest opinion, huh?" She smiles, too quickly, too casually. "You wanna say things like they are? How's this for you, then? I like you, Jonny. And I'm attracted to you. And yeah, this is a weird, intense, crazy situation we're in, and things could definitely get weird and messy, but . . . I may have woken up with my hand on your dick by accident, but it's been staying there because that's where I want it to be."

"Some truth back at ya, then: I'm having real trouble figuring out what to do, right now. I know what I want, but I also know what my conscience is telling me."

"Same here." She lifts our hands, and transfers mine to her shoulder. She withdraws her hand, and returns it to where it was, gently squeezing my aching erection. "I've never really been very good at listening to my conscience, though, Jonny."

"Me neither." I let my hand drift into the silky black mess of her hair and down to curl around her waist. "This seems a little different, though."

"How?"

I gesture around us. "Nowhere to go to be alone." I let that statement hang, for a moment. "Not here, in Ft. Lauderdale, and not for me. We want this to be more than something quick on the beach, I wouldn't know how to work that out. Things are a mess."

She sighs. "I hadn't thought about that. It feels pretty solitary, here on the beach at sunrise."

"And there's also . . ." I trail off, not sure how to phrase it.

"There's also what?"

"Ava. And Christian."

Another sigh. "Dammit." And then her eyes, so dark blue they're almost indigo, piercing, intense, cut up to mine. "What if it's not anything more than something quick on the beach?"

"I have to stay, I have to help. I have to talk to Ava, when she's ready."

"And I'm not going anywhere, because she's my sister. She's going to need me."

"Right."

She lets out a long, slow breath. "You suck, Jonny."

"I feel pretty stupid, talking you out of what you were about to do."

She laughs. "Yeah, not your best move."

I glance to where her hand is still in place, cupping me, squeezing. "Didn't seem to change much, though."

She shakes her head and traces the outline. "You said it first: I'm not very good at listening to my conscience. I know this is probably a bad idea, but I can't seem to stop myself."

"So what's going to happen?"

She shrugs. "Either one of us is going to actually stop this, or it's going to happen."

"What is?"

She reaches up and opens the button of my shorts, lowers the zipper. "This."

"Delta . . ." I murmur, knowing I should stop her.

"Jonny?"

"Why?" I ask.

"I want to."

Shit. I had whole long string of logical, convincing reasons why I have to put a stop to this, but I can't remember any of them now, because it feels like I've been hard and aching for so long I've almost forgotten what it feels like to *not* ache with need and pressure. And now she's staring up at me as she hooks her fingers into my underwear and tugs them away from my body and down, baring me.

She sucks in a breath. "Holy shit, Jonny."

I frown. "What?"

She wraps a hand around me, and it's my turn to hiss an inhalation through my teeth. "You're fucking *beautiful*, Jonny."

"I am?" My brain isn't working, due to lack of blood flow, which has, obviously, been diverted elsewhere.

"Yeah, you are."

"Been called a lot of shit in my life, never been called beautiful, though."

She laughs, squeezing me. "I mean *this*." Her hand is soft and small, pale against my darker flesh, sliding downward slowly. "The rest of you is pretty nice, too, don't get me wrong, but *this* . . . is fucking gorgeous." At the emphasized repetition, she squeezes me again.

"Oh."

She laughs again, and the sound of her laugh . . . it's music. The slow sweep of her hand on me is a sensual glide, unhurried. The sunrise is in full bloom now, bathing us in an orange glow. It's a moment that sticks in the mind, one of those moments you want to slow down and savor. For just a while, there's nothing else but her and me and the crash of the surf and the caw of the gulls and the touch of her hand, the burn of her eyes on me.

It's a sequence of stolen time. This doesn't belong to us. This moment belongs to the city that's in ruins, to the man who's like a brother to me, who deep down in my gut I feel is still alive despite the odds, and to his wife, to whom I've promised to deliver letters and the news of his disappearance. This moment belongs to the hurricane, to sorrow and destruction and loss.

Yet, I feel none of that. Not in this instant. All I feel is her, the warmth of her breath on my skin, the delicate glide of her hand on my cock, the sunrise bathing us, the cool air and the gentle wind. The promise of the moment. In the back of my head, I feel the wrongness of it, too. Too soon, too . . . not forbidden—we're nothing to each other, not in any way, so it's not forbidden in that sense. But still, somehow, this feels . . . like we *shouldn't*. But we are, and that makes it all the more exhilarating.

So far, there's not a lot of *we* in the moment, more

just her doing the touching and me letting her. But if I let her, if this happens, I'm going to touch her. Because I've been suppressing my own desire, trying to keep a handle on it. Delta is damn beautiful, and so goddamn sensual.

I've been focusing, so far, on reasons and logic, and I've been fighting myself, my mind, my body: a war between wanting to let her do this and knowing it's not right, in this moment, for reasons I can't pin down in my head.

But as she touches me, I lose all that. All of it.

I'm giving in. I can't help it. The way she's touching me is . . . there's only one word for it: sensual. Slow and soft, each movement graceful, delicate, and sure. I'm giving in to my baser feelings, my instinctive need, my body rather than my logic or my emotions.

And my body says to let this happen. To hold still and let Delta do whatever she wants, and then discover what her skin feels like. Find out if it's as soft as it looks. Find out if her tits are as big and soft and lush as they look, if her ass is as firm as it looks. If she's as responsive as she seems like she'd be, in tune with her body and what she wants and eager to get it. Neither of us are kids; neither of us are new to this.

She'd be incredible, I bet.

And I want to find out. I've been so caught up in the whole effort to dig people out that I've not allowed myself to even think about Delta like this, because there hasn't been time. But we've stolen this moment, carved it out for ourselves as dawn rises. And now that we've stolen this moment, I don't think I can go back. Now that my attraction to Delta is out of its bottle, I'm not sure I can put it back in.

There's a scuff of a footstep on the boardwalk nearby and the crackle of a radio. "No sign of him on the beach, but I know this is near where he's been camping out," a deep, rough, male voice says.

Delta freezes. Her eyes meet mine, and she's suppressing laughter, still gripping me in her fist, lip caught in her teeth, eyes twinkling.

"Keep looking then, Mike," the voice on the other end of the radio says. "Jonny's a workhorse, and he knows what he's doing. We need to get back to whoever is banging in that corner of the building. We need Jonny ASAP."

They're looking for me.

Reality douses the situation like a bucket of ice water. Delta, reluctantly and unhappily, fits me back into my shorts—a difficult thing, considering my state of arousal—zips me up, shifts upright so we're sitting side by side with our backs to the retaining wall, and covers our legs with the blanket. And now, just like that, we're two people just sitting together.

"Down here," I call out, after taking a few breaths to steady my mind.

The footsteps scuff closer, and then a pair of heavy-duty work boots appear, hanging off the edge of the retaining wall, and a uniformed police officer hops down beside me. I know him, he's Seargent Mike Harley, who's been helping coordinate and organize the efforts at Ava's building and the one next to it. Big, burly, a little overweight, just past thirty, friendly, with a blond buzz cut and the beginnings of a beard, Mike is a good man and dedicated to the relief work.

"Hey, Mike," I say, as he crouches beside me. "What's up?"

"Jonny, Delta." Mike thumbs the radio clipped to his shoulder. "Found him, Dan." To me then: "Some of the guys on the midnight shift were digging near the back corner of the next building over; that corner is pretty well caved in. They started hearing thumping, but the guys have been there for something like eighteen hours, and they're done in for the day. We were hoping you would help out. You seem to know your way around this sorta thing."

I nod. "Grew up off the coast of Nicaragua, and I've spent most of my life out there." I jut my chin at the ocean. "Seen my share of storm damage."

"So you'll help?"

I nod again. "Of course. Lead the way, Mike."

"Thank God," Mike breathes, keying his radio again. "On our way, Dan." To me, again: "Two of the guys on the midnight shift are from that building, and they say the location of the banging makes it likely it's a family they know. Mom, Dad, two little kiddies."

"It's been near on a week, Mike," I say, rising to my feet. "Doesn't seem likely."

"Rubble falls in just right, there're pockets of air, and if they have water, well . . . it's not *likely*, but it's possible."

"But a fucking week?" I shake my head. "It was blind luck we found Ava alive when we did."

"Could be nothing, could be rubble settling, or the like."

"But we gotta find out for sure," I say.

"Right," Mike says, hauling himself, with great effort, onto the boardwalk.

Delta catches at me as I turn away, glancing meaningfully at my groin. "You okay?"

I nod. "I'll live."

She tries a smile, which wobbles a little. "Rain check?"

I nod. "Bet on it."

But can the moment be repeated? I don't know.

And should it be?

Another answer I don't have.

3

I watch him vault easily up onto the boardwalk, biting my lip until it hurts. When he's out of sight, I
dissolve into barely muffled hysterical laughter, my
hands covering my face.

Holy shit, holy shit, holy shit! I'm such a slut. Did
I *really* just do that? I don't even know the man. Yeah,
sure, we've spent every moment of the last three days
essentially attached at the hip, but . . . I wouldn't know
what to do here, without him. I'm not sure why I'm still
here helping this relief effort in the first place, other than
Jonny is still here, and because there's just not space in
the over-crowded hospital for me to sit with Ava like I
really want to. I can't leave her, can't go back to Chicago,
and with the city in ruins, I can't just hang out somewhere because there's nowhere to go, it's all ruined or

underwater or without power, or just shut down. And I feel . . . connected to Jonny. Bound to him through this shared experience.

But even for me, that was bold.

I can't claim I was drunk, because obviously, I wasn't. I can't say I was half asleep and unaware of what I was doing, because I knew before I even opened my eyes what I was touching, and the state of it. I have absolutely no excuse for what I just did, other than I'm stupidly attracted to the man, and have absolutely zero percent control over my libido. Or my hands. Or my mouth.

Okay, shut up, I don't mean it like that—I didn't put my mouth on him—yet—just my hand. And only for a minute or two. Over his pants, for most of the time. And he didn't even come, which is a downer, in my book, because I really wanted to see that.

I wonder if he's a grunter when he comes. Or maybe he's a silent type, who just breathes a little heavier; God, I hope not, those types are so boring, and it's hard to tell if they liked it or not. I really hope Jonny is the vocal type, the kind of guy who makes sounds and talks to me while I'm making him come. I doubt it, though, since he's fairly taciturn.

It was such an unexpected thing, you know? I sort of slowly drifted to awareness, waking up gradually, not really understanding where I was or where I'd fallen asleep, just that I'd slept really great and was super comfy and then . . . holy fuck, that's his cock, and it's hard, and I'm touching it. And things sort of progressed from there, mostly outside my—well, not control, exactly, but . . . God, I don't know. I knew exactly what I was doing, and I *could* have stopped, as in, my self-control is perfectly functional, thank you. I just don't possess much will to stop myself from doing something that feels good in the moment, even if I know, mentally, that it's not the greatest of ideas.

But it's a bad, bad plan to get involved with him, because . . . um.

Because I'm a single mom, number one.

Number two, he's a nomad. We've talked about his travels quite a bit, and though he hasn't come right out and said so, it's clear he's a vagabond, with no home and no family and no ties to anywhere.

Number three, I have two settings when it comes to men: Fuck-and-Flee, and Stage Five Clinger. Reason 3-A: it seems we're both slated to be in the area for some time—Jonny because he owes some sort of duty to Chris to talk to Ava and give her some letters or something, and me because she's my sister, and she's alone and she lost her home and she's hurt and her husband is missing, presumed dead—and pulling a fuck-and-flee with a guy I then run the risk of having to see again, perhaps frequently, is a bad idea. Reason 3-B: getting involved with a guy, who, per reason number two, is just going to leave and not come back, like . . . ever, and letting myself go all Stage Five Clinger on him is, clearly, the very height of stupidity.

Number four, he's Christian's best friend, and they're clearly very close, and Ava is Christian's wife, but they're estranged, or they were. It is just a bad idea because it smacks of complication and entanglement.

Well, maybe number four might be a bit of a stretch but still, I have three good reasons.

But I really want to, and he's hot, and he's mysterious, and he's forbidden in a weird sort of way, and he's got a seriously beautiful penis.

God, this is complicated.

It *was* hot, though. Witty banter, a nice build up.

The fact is . . . I'm horny; that's just the long and short of it. I could make a pros and cons list a mile long, but the fact is I've been on a dry spell lately, leaving me all kinds of worked up. Work has been crazy lately, and I had to replace the muffler on my car, get new calipers and pads, and fix the serpentine belt, all of which cost enough that I've had to work double shifts the last few weeks just to pay the credit card back down to a non-heart-attack-inducing level.

But none of that negates the fact that I am simply horny, and that does not portend good things in terms of my ability to resist a man like Jonny.

What do I do?

Hell if I know.

God, I do want him, though. And now that I've had my hand on him, I want him even more. But, for the reasons stated above, I'm going to get hurt. Generations of women before me have come to realize you can't keep a man with the wanderlust bug chained at home in one place. Not without ruining his spirit.

I groan out loud and put the entire conundrum out of my head, because I'm going in circles—*do I, don't I?*

Enough, Delta. Move on. Take things as they come. If you sleep with him, you sleep with him. Enjoy it, relish the time and the experience, and know you'll have to let him go when it's over. Understand you're going to get hurt, accept it, prepare for it, and don't hold it against him.

With those instructions firmly stamped on my brain, I stand up, brush the sand off my legs, fold the blanket, pile the supplies he's gathered into a neat stack, and climb up the retaining wall to see where I can be put to work.

I spy Jonny and a group of ten other men standing on a pile of rubble, deep in the back corner of the partially-collapsed building next to Ava's. Someone has brought one of those big yellow construction machines with the arm and the scooper—hell if I know what it's called, though Alex would know and would tell you everything about in under a minute. They've driven it close to the building, extended the arm close to the men digging out the rubble. The men toss the brick and stones and pipes and various pieces of debris and detritus into the scoop and every once in a while, the machine pivots to dump the rubble into a pile off to one side and then pivots again to return to its original position. I wonder, at first, why they don't just use the scooper to dig at the pile, but then I realize that if there *are* people alive under all that debris, the scooper might hurt them or dislodge things in such a way as to crush them, leaving the rescue workers with no option but to dig by hand.

I find a group of other women working under a makeshift tent. They're sorting supplies brought in by some aid organization or another, and I spend the next several hours sorting through flats of bottled water, boxes of canned food, and crates of medical supplies. Every once in a while, I steal a glance over at Jonny working with the men; he's tirelessly hauling at the debris, even directing others where to pick at so as not to dislodge the rubble. He's filthy by now, streaked with dirt, his hair messy and filthy from his dirty hands scraping through it. He's shirtless, his already dark Latin skin burned darker by endless hours in the sun at sea.

He's a beast, is what he is.

I know he's a few years older than me, with sexy hints of silver creeping in at the temples, and in the stubble that's pretty much a beard by now. But *damn*, he's in amazing shape. He's not ripped and cut like an Instagram model, which is nice to look at of course, but doesn't seem real. No, Jonny is the perfect *real* man, in my opinion. Solidly muscled, with thick pecs and toned, hard, round biceps, a trim waist and a hint of a six-pack, but there's some evidence on his body that he enjoys life and loves food and likes to drink, but still takes care of himself.

His body is that of a man who has spent his whole life hauling at ropes and carrying supplies and doing hard physical work all day every day, keeping him naturally fit, rather than the carved-from-marble perfection of a man who spends all day in the gym.

Now, I'm lucky if I can keep even a so-so looking guy's interest for more than a couple dates and a quick fuck or two in his dingy-ass apartment after drinks at the bar before going home to pick up Alex from Mrs. Allen's apartment. And even that is getting old and unsatisfying. Although, really, that's always *been* old and unsatisfying for me. I've always wanted more—shit, I *still* want more now, but I'm at the stage and the age where I'm beginning to despair I'll ever find more with anyone. I mean, I'm thirty-eight, a single mother working dead-end jobs, no future, no meaningful career or accomplishments. Sure, I had a couple songs bought by some country music stars, but even that didn't pan out.

A surprised shout from one of the men shakes me out of my thoughts, and everyone in the vicinity stops working to watch, or to hustle over and see how they can help. There's a crowd on the pile, and Mike the police officer gently but firmly guides them back.

I find myself in that crowd, at the very front, standing precariously on a pile of broken cinderblocks nearby, watching as Jonny works feverishly. He's on his hands and knees, picking gingerly at the debris, carefully removing cinderblocks and pipes and chunks of drywall and setting them aside. He leans farther into the hole he's creating, until his entire upper half is bent forward into the hole, reaching back to hand chunks and bits to whomever is close enough to take them from him. And then, moving as slowly and carefully as if crossing thin, cracking ice, he lowers himself into the gaping maw in the rubble, vanishing completely.

The gathered crowd is utterly hushed and still.

I hear a noise from the hole, Jonny's voice saying something I can't make out, and one of the other men nearby reaches in and hauls out a form, a body. A still, limp, female. Her arms dangle, her feet trail listlessly. The man carries her with exquisite care, stepping down the pile with her in his arms. He's mid-fifties, muscular but with a slight belly, grizzled and graying, wearing a sleeveless shirt with the logo of a construction company on it. His face is shut down, hard, solemn. His eyes are locked on the woman in his arms, who, as he passes me with her, I see is still alive, but only barely. Her eyes flit sluggishly, and one hand has something clutched in it, a photograph. She's young, Hispanic, and beautiful. And very clearly slipping all too quickly into death. She has moments left. She's been holding on, desperately. She abruptly jerks in her savior's arms, twisting, moaning, reaching frantically, calling out names.

"He's gettin' 'em, honey, he's getting 'em. Good ol'

Jonny's gettin' 'em, okay? Settle for me, settle. Calm, calm." His voice is as rough and grizzled as he is, and it's clear the woman doesn't understand.

I turn back to look at the hole, and Jonny is handing up a second body, and a third. These are much, much smaller. Children. They're alive, squirming, crying weakly, shielding their eyes from the bright Florida sun as men take them from Jonny and carry them down the pile of rubble. I think Jonny is going to emerge, but he doesn't. He stays down for a long few moments, and then emerges slowly, a burden over one shoulder. He refuses to let anyone take the burden from him as he climbs out. The burden is another body. This one, like the woman, is an adult. A male. Totally limp, bent in half over Jonny's shoulder, dangling, lifeless. The father. Young, Hispanic, and handsome.

Jonny carries him off the rubble pile. Joining him at the makeshift tent, I see that Jonny is . . . devastated. It is the only word I know for the expression on his face. He gently deposits the male form onto the ground, falling to his knees to allow the limp body to come rest on the grass. There's no sign of serious injury, and it looks to me as if the man hasn't been dead long, but he is very clearly gone now.

The woman, lying on a fold-out military surplus cot nearby, weakly lifts a hand toward the man, her husband. She's weeping, or she would be if she weren't utterly dehydrated. Her lips are cracked and shriveled, her skin papery and pale. She's muttering in Spanish, and after laying the man onto the grass, Jonny scoots across to sit beside her. He takes her hand and whispers to her in Spanish, shaking his head. The woman is wracked with shuddering sobs, but she's too weak even for that. She says something else to Jonny, who twists, spies the two children—a boy and a girl—being tended to by Red Cross volunteers. He points at them, talking to the woman. She reaches for them, tries to sit up, but can't. Jonny scoops his hand under her head and helps her sit up so she can see her children, only a few feet away. They are both being fitted with an IV bag, as is the woman, while Jonny continues to whisper to her.

Not knowing what else to do, I sit beside Jonny on the ground beside the woman. He acknowledges me with a glance and a nod, and then returns his attention to the woman, speaking to her in Spanish. She mutters something every once in a while, and Jonny responds. He holds her hand. A doctor appears from somewhere, haggard looking, exhausted. I recognize him from the hospital, and it's clear he's been working nonstop like everyone else, with little food and less rest. He examines the woman briefly, but his expression is grave.

I overhear him speaking to the nurses. "Push IV fluids, but that's about it, I'm afraid. Anyone's guess, at this point. She may be too far gone, but if she's a fighter, she may pull through. No injuries I can see, no trauma. Just severe dehydration, possibly some lung damage from inhaling debris dust. Push fluids, that's all I can say." He sighs heavily. "It's in God's hands now."

And then he's gone, checking the two little children.

I sit with Jonny for hours. I might be needed elsewhere, but there's no chance of me leaving him, not now.

Jonny never moves. Never lets go of of the woman's hand. Sometimes, he talks to her in Spanish, sometimes I think maybe he's singing to her, but it's too low for me to hear even sitting beside him. I doze off again, sitting up beside him.

I'm woken by a scuffed footstep and quiet voices. Jonny is asleep, sitting up, head lolled forward, still holding the woman's hand. It's a male Red Cross volunteer, a penlight in one hand, shielding the glow with his palm— he's young, with a shaggy blond beard and world-weary blue eyes.

It's the deep dark of past midnight, cool air stirring, stars shining beyond the tent. With so much of the city without power, there's less light pollution, so the stars are more visible. The male nurse touches two fingers just beneath the woman's nose, and his frown deepens. He touches the same two fingers to the side of her throat, holds them there a few moments, and then sighs sadly. He thumbs the switch to close the IV line and gently removes the needle.

I touch Jonny's shoulder. "Hey. Jonny."

He starts awake. "*Que*? Um—what?" He straightens, blinks at me, and then at the volunteer lifting the IV bag free of the hook. "What're you . . . where are you taking that?" He sounds stubborn. Petulant, almost.

The volunteer doesn't quite look at Jonny. "She's gone, man. I'm sorry. The fluids are needed elsewhere, there's not enough to go around."

Jonny is silent a long moment. "She's not gone." He shifts, leans forward, touches fingers to her neck. "She's not gone. Where's the doctor?"

I wrap an arm around him. "Jonny. You did everything you could."

He shakes me off. "No. No. I got her out. I got her kids out. He was . . . he was already dead when I got down there, but I got her out."

I feel a hot lump in my throat. "You did everything you could, Jonny. No one could have done anything more. You've done more than . . . more than anyone."

He shakes his head, murmuring in Spanish too low and too rapid for me to make out, and then louder in English. "She was—she needs the IV. The doctor, he said—he said to push fluids. She'll—her babies—no, no."

I wrap my arm around him again, try to pull him away. "Jonny, there wasn't . . . there wasn't anything anyone could have done." I tug at him, but he's immovable. "Jonny, come on. You've done enough for today. Come on."

"Hours, I—I dug for hours. If—maybe if I'd dug faster, or started sooner, maybe they'd—they both might still be—" He shakes his head, making a keening sound in the back of his throat that is . . . it's utterly heartbreaking. "I have to—I have to—" He lurches to his feet, staggering out of the tent and toward the ruined building.

I follow him at a run and catch up to him. I cut in front of him and stop with my hands on his chest. "Jonny, stop. Please, please, Jonny, please, just stop for a second."

He blinks at me as if now realizing I'm here; he's flashing back, I think, to some past trauma. "I have to go back. I have to help. I have to save them."

I move slowly, unsure of his mental state at the moment, gathering him into a hug. He's stiff, tensed, breathing heavily. Shaking his head. Hands fisted at his sides, eyes wild, now.

"Hush, Jonny. You've done so much. You've been here, digging for days. You've saved so many lives, Jonny." I hold him, and he lets me, but he doesn't move.

"I—I didn't save them."

"You tried."

He shakes his head. *"Mi hermana, mi madre. Mi sobrino . . ."* he whispers. *"No pude salvarlos . . ."*

I've worked in enough restaurants and bars with Spanish-speakers to have picked up a little Spanish over the years to understand what he said—*my sister, my mother. My nephew. I could not save them.*

"You tried, Jonny. You did everything you could."

He sucks in a deep, deep breath. Holds it. Lets it out slowly, with a broken shudder. "Never—it's . . . it's never enough."

"Can we go to our spot on the beach, Jonny?" I pull him in that direction. "Let's go sit down for a minute, okay?"

"Her babies." He blinks, starting to come out of his thoughts. "I have to—I need to see them."

"Okay, let's go see them."

So we go back to the tent, to a pair of cots that are much too big for the tiny, orphaned bodies in them. A four-year-old boy and a three-year-old girl. IV lines are taped to their forearms. They're sleeping.

A female Red Cross volunteer nearby shushes us softly. "They're exhausted, the poor things," she whispers, ushering us away a few feet. "Poor, poor little dears." She's mid-forties, thin, efficient, and warm, a woman who has spent her whole life as a nurse.

"They're going to be okay?" Jonny asks.

The nurse nods. "Yes. They'll be just fine." She glances at the now-empty cot. "Such a tragedy about their parents, though."

"What will happen, now?" Jonny's gaze stays on the children.

"Oh, social services will take them, eventually. Things are such a mess right now, though. Who knows when that will happen?"

"Until then?"

She shrugs. "We make sure they get fed. Someone will have to tell them about their parents. We will all stick together and help out." Another shrug and a sigh.

"That's what we do when tragedies happen."

"Look for the helpers," I put in. "Mr. Rogers once said that as a kid, whenever something bad happened on TV, his mother would tell him to look for the helpers; there would always be people helping."

The nurse nods. "Yes. Well, we're all the helpers now, aren't we?"

Jonny rubs his face. "I'll talk to them when they wake up. I don't think they speak any English."

"I'll personally come find you when they wake up, okay?" The nurse pats him on the shoulder. "Go rest, okay? You need it."

Jonny trudges away, and I follow him. We go to our little nest—well, *his* little nest, which I've somehow turned into *our* little nest. I wonder if I should give him space or stay close? I don't know. This is utterly uncharted territory for me, dealing with such raw, intense emotion. Jonny is clearly reliving some past horror, collating that with this current situation, and his placid and seemingly imperturbable demeanor is suddenly cracked, and I'm seeing through to the depth of the man behind it.

He slips off the boardwalk and collapses into the sand, sitting abruptly, as if he's suddenly too weak to move. I sit beside him. Shoulder to shoulder, hip to hip.

"Jonny, I—" I break off with a sigh, unsure what I'm trying to say. "I'm here."

He nods heavily, staring out at the rippling sea, the moon a bright disc painting a path on the water, stars infinite and scintillating. "Thank you."

"Do you . . . do you still want my company? Or would you rather be alone?" I ask, my voice hesitant.

He digs his fingers into the sand, wiggling them deeper and deeper under until he's buried up to the wrists. "Don't go. Please." He says this without looking at me.

"I just . . . I've sort of latched onto you since I got here, and—" I pause, hesitating, and then voice my deepest doubts. "I don't want to . . . overwhelm you, or overstay my welcome with you. If you know what I mean."

He shakes his head. "Having you around, the last few days—it's . . . it's been good. I've done this before, helped people after a hurricane. It's never easy. But with Chris missing and Ava still in the hospital, I wouldn't . . . it would be harder if I was alone. I'm usually happier being alone, but after what I've been through the last few weeks?" He shrugs, shakes his head again. "No, Delta, if I have to be here, doing this, I'm very, very glad to be here, doing it with you."

I smile helplessly, my heart thrilling and lurching into my throat. "Same." I pause. "This hurricane . . . I don't know much about hurricanes in general, but it seems like this one came out of nowhere."

He nods. "It did. This was a very powerful out-of-season storm, and it just cropped up out of nowhere and hit like a freight train. Me and Chris were on the outer edge of it as it was developing over across the Atlantic, off the southern coast of Africa. It was nice and clear, smooth sailing, and then . . . *bam*, it hit. We didn't have a chance to try to get away from it or go back to port and ride it out. It overtook us, smacked us to shit, and . . . that was it. Chris went overboard, and I managed to stay with the boat until Dom rescued me, which was a miracle in and of itself, honestly."

There's another long silence between us.

He finally twists his head to look at me, and our faces are so close, too close. "About this morning, Delta . . ."

I interrupt him. "We don't have to talk about it."

He doesn't look away, and I can't either—I'm somehow just incapable of breaking the eye contact. "In a way, I'm glad of the interruption."

I blink at him, surprised. "You . . . you are?" I'm not sure if I'm supposed to be hurt or insulted or just baffled, and I go with baffled. "Why? I mean, it can't have been comfortable, getting stopped when you were obviously, you know, so close."

He nods. "Well, yeah. That part sucked a little. But . . ." He pauses, his eyes searching mine. "That was a weird situation, and if something were to happen between you and me, Delta, I don't want it be by accident, you know? Also, I feel like that would have been . . . one-sided. And that's not how I do things."

"I'm not the type of woman to keep count, Jonny," I tell him. "I do what I want, what feels good. And I may not know much about you, but I get the sense you're not the type of man who'd leave his partner wanting or frustrated."

"Hell, no," he says, and somehow we've shifted even closer to each other. "Never. That's why I'm glad things happened like they did. Because I'm not sure how I would have given back what you were giving. We ain't exactly in a private place, you know?"

I nod, sighing. "Yeah, I see what you're saying."

He eyes me, reading me. "But?"

"But . . ." I laugh ruefully. "I don't like leaving things unfinished. And this morning, it may have started by accident, but . . . I was doing what I wanted to do, because I wanted to do it. Not with any expectation of getting something in return. So things just feel . . . I don't know. Unfinished."

He's quiet for a while. "I hope you can understand this, Delta, but . . . I'm not in a place right now where I can . . ." He shrugs, and it's obvious he's deeply uncomfortable saying this. "I can't go there. Not tonight. Not after"—he waves behind us, at the medical tent—"not after all that."

I nod and look away. "I totally get that."

"It's not that I don't want to, Delta."

I smile at him, trying to seem reassuring, which is hard because the welter of emotions running through me certainly contains a strong note of disappointment. "I understand. Absolutely."

He's still so close to me, his body and mine touching all along one side. His face is near enough to mine that a tilt and a slight lean, and we could kiss.

Not that he's going to do that.

I'm not either, obviously.

Kissing him? That'd be . . . ooh boy, that would certainly be a step in the direction of Stage Five Clinger territory, which as previously established, would be phenomenally stupid.

So, yeah, duh. Not kissing him.

And he's not kissing me, because he's not looking for a clinger. Shit, he may not even be looking for a hook-up, you know? I mean, maybe he's the type who would have let me jerk him off, but because it was happening and not because he'd been looking for it, or had any intention of reciprocating, much less letting things progress into actual sex.

His eyes are flitting back and forth, searching mine. And his head is tilting. And he's leaning.

He's *leaning*.

What?

No, no, no—No! If he kisses me, I'm gonna freak out.

Holy shit, he's kissing me.

Is this real? I think it is. He's leaning in, his body is angling toward mine, and his lips are sliding softly against mine, and now his hand is cupping the side of my face, and I feel my eyes closing and I feel his mouth on mine, and I let myself indulge in this. Remind myself, mentally, that this doesn't mean anything. He's kissing me carefully, delving slowly into it. Which is even more confusing. Because if this had been one of those hard and urgent *I just can't help myself* kind of blindingly passionate kisses, I would have just chalked it up to hormones and the intensity of the moment or something, but this kiss is . . . it's intentional.

My heart is pounding, and my hands are shaking as I feel myself falling into the kiss. I can't *not* kiss him back. God, I want this. I want him to be kissing me intentionally, and I want it to devolve into something more, because I just want him. All of him, as much as I can get. I'm anticipating being hurt, so I may as well get as much pleasure as I can out of things before that happens. Right?

But holy shit, his kiss is intoxicating. So slow. Warm. Gentle, but insistent. His mouth is firm, and damp. He's leading this kiss, his hand is on my cheek and jaw and the back of my neck, and he's leaning into me, and all I can do it kiss him back.

I'm breathless.

An ache begins, throbbing low in my core as his kiss intensifies and the heat rises between us, and I'm losing myself in it. I let myself just . . . enjoy it. I want him to lay me back in the sand, but I'm not going to push it. I bury a hand in his hair, and I feel his tongue trace my upper lip, and then his other hand, once bracing his weight in the sand, wraps around my lower back and pulls me closer. My breasts smash against his chest, and I hear a soft whimpering moan, and I realize it's me making that sound.

It was a breathy, needy, erotic moan; do I really sound like that? I'm not sure I've ever made that noise before.

And the tingles. God, the tingles. It's gone beyond mere tingling, now, though. It's . . . a hum. A vibration, deep inside me, from the soul outward.

He breaks the kiss, finally, and I'm left gasping, and my lips are tingling, and I still have my hand in his silky black hair.

"Jonny, I—" I refuse to let go. I want *more*. "I'm even more confused, now."

"I know. I'm sorry."

"You said you weren't in the right place for . . ." I shrug, wave a hand. "That."

"I know. But I just . . . I had to kiss you." He shakes his head, as if at a loss for words. "I don't know. I just had to kiss you."

I'm shaking all over. My core is throbbing. The kiss was . . . it was fucking intense, and I'm turned on now, and I don't think he's going to take it beyond that.

I'm upset, and I'm not sure why.

I'm frustrated, and I'm confused. He's giving me all kinds of mixed signals. I don't know what he wants, if he wants me, or if he doesn't. The man is . . . *opaque* as a person. I cannot read him. Right now, he's frowning slightly and his chest is rising and falling heavily as if that kiss left him as off-balance as it did me, but he's not kissing me, and he didn't try to further it, didn't touch me, didn't seem to be inviting anything more than just the kiss.

What are we, fourteen, when kisses are just kisses, and not a gateway into sex?

No one I've ever met an adult who *just* kisses someone except maybe on the first date, and they sure as hell wouldn't kiss like *that*.

So . . . what the hell?

Also, I'm turned on, as in my sex drive is going haywire, and I fucking want Jonny, I want him to touch me, I want to feel his cock in my hand again, and I want to finish what I started. I want to make him come, and I want to feel his hands on me, or his mouth on me, and I want to come, and I want to fuck him. I'm so goddamn horny it's stupid, and I don't trust myself.

I'm sitting here on the beach in the middle of the night, trembling all over. I'm so worked up and turned on, and this man is just staring at me, one hand on my lower back, the other still on my face, and I'm gripping his hair at the back of his head like we're still kissing, but we're not, we're just staring into each other's eyes and somehow just completely failing to be able to read each other.

If I don't get out of here, I'm going to do something stupid, like grab his dick and suck him off, and then, despite my earlier claim to not need or expect reciprocation, I'm going to shove his hand or his mouth between my thighs and make it abundantly clear I want him to give me an orgasm.

So, instead of doing any of that, I abruptly stand up. "I—I have to . . ." I turn away. Shaking, thighs quaking, frustration boiling through me, and need unraveling inside me. "I have to go. I have to go."

And I run.

I've done a lot of running in my life. When emotions come into play, when things start turning into something that might mean something, I run. When life hands me a situation I don't know to deal with, I deal with it by running. When it became clear music wasn't happening in Nashville, I ran. When I found out I was pregnant, I took Tom's money and I ran.

This is the first time, though, I've run away before sleeping with a man; usually, the running happens *after*. This is me running preemptively.

This time, though, I literally run. Which, I don't really do, like ever. I do yoga, I lift weights, I do spin classes . . . I do *not* run. My tits are too big, for one thing. And I just hate it, for another. But this time . . . I run. I jog along the sand, my tits punching me in the face with each step, since I'm wearing that stupid push-up bra I wear at work since it gets me better tips. But the bra is a piece of shit and doesn't do shit for support, so I'm flopping and bouncing like a *Baywatch* slow-mo shoot gone wrong. I run, because if I don't, I'm going to give in and go Stage Five Clinger on Jonny, because he's amazing and sexy and compassionate and deep and mysterious, and I've never met a man like him, one who moves my soul *and* my libido.

He obviously doesn't want me, and I'm not going to embarrass myself any more than I have already. I could end up doing something desperate and idiotic, and if I want to retain *any* of my dignity, I have to get away from Jonny Nuñez.

I run down the beach, not sure where I'm going, just . . . *away.*

A glow down the beach lures me, the flickering orange of a bonfire. There's music—a guitar, someone expertly using upturned buckets as drums, and it sounds like someone is playing a cello. It's beautiful, impromptu, improvised music. It's been so long since I played or sang around anyone else. I let the music pull me in and take me over, and I let the music breathe through my soul.

I've been Mommy for so long, I've been just surviving for so long . . .

But this . . . this draws me in.

I approach, slowing to a walk. It's a massive bonfire, the flames flickering ten or twelve feet in the air, and there are about twenty or thirty people sitting around it, in pairs or in groups, talking, laughing. The musicians are all sitting together in a shallow semi-circle, well away from the fire, almost in the shadows, their backs to the sea. Informal, just a group of like-minded individuals making the most of the moment. The guitarist is a fit older man, early to mid sixties, with long salt-and-pepper hair tied back, and a graying black beard. He's wearing a loud Hawaiian shirt and board shorts. He's not exactly good-looking, but not unattractive, either. The cellist is a woman in her late twenties, reddish-blonde hair, pretty but plain. The percussionist is a young white man in his late teens or very early twenties, blond hair in long dreadlocks, a scraggly beard, wearing jeans cut raggedly just below the knee, no shirt, heavily tattooed. They are each phenomenal musicians, but together, they're . . . just amazing. The melody they're playing is a familiar one that I cannot quite place, mournful, haunting.

I hesitate on the outskirts of the ring of light, listening. Letting the music seep into my soul.

God, I miss music.

When I was young, music was literally *everything* to me. I believed in myself. I practiced obsessively. I wrote hundreds of songs. I did open mic nights all over Florida as a teenager, honing my craft by developing my guitar skills, my singing, and my song writing. I moved to Nashville within weeks of turning eighteen and busted my ass making ends meet while trying to make it as a singer-songwriter. I did everything I could to make it as a musician—including blowing a record producer once, which I'm not proud of, but hey, it was when I was beginning to realize a music career wasn't going to happen for me, and it was a last ditch, desperate attempt to keep the dream alive.

I had fucking *talent*, too. I really did. But sometimes, talent, looks, and skill just aren't enough. Sometimes, life just . . . bites you in the ass.

Then I had Alex, and I've been devoting myself into raising him, keeping him clothed and educated and fed and safe, and I haven't had time to do anything except dick around with my guitar, alone, late at night, more out of boredom and loneliness and nostalgia than anything else.

But standing here on the beach with so much sadness inside me percolating and simmering from the days of caring for wounded people, from hearing someone weep at night because a loved one was found dead, and from watching people sort through the rubble of a community's collective lives . . . yet the music is a salve.

I just stand on the edge of the light and close my eyes and listen, soaking it up.

The song ends, and there's a moment of discussion, and then the guitarist starts in on "Jolene" by Dolly Parton. And I'm immediately thrown back twenty years to when I was a fresh young talent brand new to Nashville and full of dreams, taking on enormous songs like "Jolene" in the honky-tonks on Lower Broadway. God, I used to fucking *slay* this song.

I feel my fingers moving on my thigh, mimicking the chords.

The drummer picks up the beat, and they jam for a minute, the drummer and the guitarist, drawing out the intro. The cellist just listens for a while; I think she knows the song, but she's figuring out how to join in. There she goes—she's doing the violin part. Her playing lends the song a deeper sorrow and longing and gravitas.

The guitarist starts singing the verses, and his voice is rough and gravelly, but in tune and compelling. I can't help but sing along. I try to keep quiet, knowing I've not been invited into this moment, but unable to help myself from joining in.

The guitarist hears me first, his gaze sweeping the darkness until it finds me, and he smiles encouragingly and jerks his head to indicate I should join in. So I do. I sit crosslegged between the guitarist and the cellist, and I find the harmony. It all comes rushing back, a torrent of memory. The music has me in its grip, and I sing that song with everything I've got.

There's scattered applause when the music ends, and the guitarist smiles at me. "Well, damn, girl," he says, in a slow southern drawl. "You've got a mighty fine voice."

I smile and shrug. "Thanks."

He introduces himself as Rob, the cellist is Elaine, and the drummer is Corey, and I offer them my first name, and receive a flurry of other names from the others around us, and suddenly everyone seems so genuine and friendly and welcoming, and my heart is thrilling and filling and swelling.

Rob flicks a finger at my hands, clutched in front of me. "Saw your hands as you were singing, looks like you know how to play."

I shrug again. "I used to play. Still do, a little bit."

He hands me his guitar. "Take it away, sugar."

I take the guitar, and it settles into place perfectly. I stroke the strings, find a chord, and strum. God, the voice of this instrument is . . . it's like honey. I note the maker's name on the headstock: Martin. Shit, no wonder this guitar sounds so good. It's very old, impeccably maintained, and probably worth a fortune.

I search inside myself for something to play, but nothing comes to mind, and I know myself well enough to know the only way I'll find the right song is to let it emerge on its own. So I let my fingers do the talking. A chord, another, some idle strumming, learning the personality of this incredible guitar.

Soon enough, the melody to "The Sound of Silence" by Simon & Garfunkel emerges. My dad was big on the classics from when he was younger: Simon and Garfunkel, Dolly Parton, James Taylor, Cat Stevens, Carly Simon, that kind of thing. It was what we grew up on, because it was what he'd listen to all day every day. He'd be out in the garage, tinkering with his old Camaro, and he'd have a tape on, and I'd sit and listen to the music and watch him tinker. Ava never understood why I'd sit out there for so long, on that old stool by Dad's cluttered workbench, watching him tinker and listening to the music. But I just loved it. I loved the music, the smell of the grease and the heat in the old garage, and the way

Dad would sing along under his breath. Ava was always more interested in reading the latest book or magazine and going to the mall with her friends. Me? I just liked listening to music with Dad. Later, those songs I grew up listening to became my go-to cover songs, because I knew them all backward and forward. They were what I learned to play the guitar on, and when I did my first open mic night, it was "Cat's in the Cradle" by Harry Chapin. When I booked my first paying gig, I started with a James Taylor song and ended with a Carly Simon song, and did everything I could think of in the hour and a half in between. I was booked for a return gig the next week based on that performance. Even after I had a full set list of my own original material, I'd still throw in covers of the songs I cut my teeth on.

Which is why Simon and Garfunkel is what comes out when I start playing. It's a comfort song, that one. Dad's favorite song. The first song I ever learned to play. I'm back in Florida, feeling the sea breeze in my hair, and I have a guitar in my hands and a song in my heart and, for a moment, at least, I feel a measure of something like happiness.

Corey and Elaine fill in their parts, and I let Simon and Garfunkel flow out of me. Rob harmonizes with me, and I'm transported, flown away to that place in my soul where music lives. My talent is rusty from disuse, but this is wetting it, feeding it, greasing it until the cogs churn effortlessly again.

The song ends, but Elaine keeps playing, shifting into something else, her own melody, maybe. Corey adds a slow beat, and I listen for a moment, but my hands know what to do, even if my head doesn't. I play with them, add a simple, repeating refrain. Rob leans backward against the wall of the boardwalk and comes back with a mandolin, and then layers in his own contribution. We just play, then, the four of us. It's a simple song we're playing, but it's lovely and delicate and somehow joyful. Hopeful, in a time of hardship. I look around at the people by the fire, and there are bandages and casts and bruises, sorrow and worry lines, fear, sadness, anger. And our music, it's a moment of light in the darkness.

I see Jonny, at the edge of the light, arms crossed over his chest, watching me play.

I lose track of time after that. Jonny just watches, and more people filter in and some leave, and there's someone with a little camera, recording us. We play for hours, Rob with his mandolin and me with Rob's gorgeous Martin, Elaine with her cello, and Corey with his bucket drums. We play The Counting Crows, Michael Jackson, Crosby Stills and Nash, Jonny Cash, Alan Jackson, The Black Keys, The White Stripes, and if one of us doesn't know a song, we improvise. People sing along, and some dance, and others make out, and there's a sense of camaraderie between us all, born in the ruins of the hurricane and brought to life by the music, the shared moment of enjoyment when all else is so dark and painful.

Eventually, Corey says he's beat and has to sleep, and Elaine just blinks sleepily and wanders away with her cello and bow, and now it's just me and Rob.

I hand Rob his guitar back. "Thanks for letting me play. She's a beautiful instrument."

Rob takes it and strokes the strings. "She sure is, ain't she? Ol' Gloria and me, we've been makin' music together more'n thirty years, now." He nods at me. "You're a fine hand with the six-string, Delta, and you got a voice like an angel. Pleasure to jam with you, sweetheart."

I smile self-consciously at his compliment. "Thanks, Rob. Did me a world of good to play and sing again. Been a while."

"I think there's talk of another fire tomorrow," Rob says. "Swing on by and we'll jam again. I know Gloria will be lookin' forward to it, and so will I." He eyes the shadows, and sees Jonny. "Looks like a fella's waitin' for you."

I stand up. "I'd love to play with Gloria again," I say. "Thanks again."

"It was my pleasure, and I do mean that. Hope we see you tomorrow night."

I stroll away from the fire, past Jonny without slowing down or acknowledging him, because I don't know what to say or how to act around him. He catches up in a few easy strides and walks beside me in silence. I walk straight past his little nest, ignoring him still.

A quarter mile later he finally breaks the silence,

trotting around in front of me to force me to a halt.

"Delta."

I cross my arms over my chest. "Jonny."

He sighs, as if hunting for the right words. "I don't know . . . *dios mio*, this is hard." He starts again. "I don't know how to navigate this, Delta. I'm a sailor, that's what I do, I sail. I can circumnavigate the globe without a chart or GPS, using the old ways, but this thing, you and me? I can't make my way through it. I'm not trying to hurt or confuse you, I just . . . I don't know what I'm doing."

I laugh. "I can't even navigate Chicago without GPS, and I've lived there for years. So . . . I don't know how to navigate this either." I shrug. "Maybe there's nothing to navigate."

"You don't think so?"

I lift my hands palms up. "Hell if I know, Jonny. I mean, part of me wants there to be, but honestly, no, I don't think there is." I let out a long sigh. "I have to . . . I have to figure out where I'm going next, what I'm doing. I can't stay out here on the beach, digging through rubble. I have a son who needs me. I have bills to pay. I have a life. I have a sister who's about to get out of the hospital, and she has no home, nowhere to go, and her husband is missing, probably dead. So no, I don't think there's anything to navigate."

"It kinda feels like there could be, though." Jonny steps closer to me.

"Don't, Jonny." I back away. "Yeah, it does kind of feel like there could be, but feelings fade, don't they? I'm sure you've had feelings for someone before, but it's never kept you in one place, has it? This isn't going to be any different. Like I said, I have a son who needs me, so even if I wanted to, I can't just . . . go gallivanting across the world on a sailboat."

I wave a hand at the sea. "Your life is out there"—I wave behind me, at the land—"and mine is out there. It was nice spending time with you, and it was amazing getting to know you, and I'm for sure gonna regret this later because I'm crazy attracted to you, but . . . there's nothing there, Jonny. Nothing real and lasting."

He sighs. "That's not how I wanted this to go."

"Me either." I shake my head and sigh. "But . . . I don't think there's any other way it could have gone."

A long beat of silence. "I'm gonna go visit Ava tomorrow. I have to give her the box from Christian."

"I'll go with you. She's really going to need me when you're done."

He nods heavily. "Yes. I think you're right." He steps backward, away from me. "So . . . where will you sleep?"

I gesture at the sand by the edge of the boardwalk. "Here, I guess."

He shakes his head and rolls his eyes. "Don't. That's dumb."

"I can sleep fine in the sand."

"We'll keep our distance, if that's what you need. But

staying way over here all by yourself? It's not safe." He steps toward me again. "Law and order tends to break down at times like these."

"I'll be fine." I'm totally lying: the idea of sleeping in the bare sand, alone, no blankets, no one around? It's utterly terrifying.

He frowns at me. "What are you afraid of, Delta? What do you think I'm going to do?"

I laugh, an amused, sarcastic bark. "It's not *you* I'm afraid of, Jonny."

His frown deepens. "Then what?"

I shake my head, not wanting to answer. But I do. "Myself. I'm afraid of what *I'll* do."

Jonny takes my hand and leads me back towards his nest. "Come on, Delta. It'll be fine. We're both adults. Nothing will happen." Another few steps. "I'm not letting you sleep out here alone. It's not safe."

He's not safe either, but in a totally different way.

I go with him, knowing deep in my gut that this is going to lead to me doing something stupid. Because . . . hello, this is me. I specialize in making stupid decisions that are bound to accomplish nothing but hurt me and make my life more difficult.

We lay down in the little nest of blankets, in the divot we've made in the sand. We lie close, but not *too* close. Spooning, but not touching in anyway. Just sleeping. Neither of us says anything as we fall asleep because, really, there's nothing to say.

Once again, I wake up in extreme discomfort. This time, though, Delta isn't lying on me, so I can slip out of the blankets and drain my bladder into the sand a few dozen feet away, and then slip back into the blankets. I'm careful to keep my distance from her, but it's difficult. I want to be closer. I want to spoon up behind her, hold her close. Inhale her scent. Feel her body, touch her curves. I want to hear her moan again. The way she moaned last night when I kissed her. Shit. I almost exploded when I heard that little sound, and all we were doing was kissing.

It's well before dawn; the sky is still mostly dark and only beginning to be tinged with gray. I sink back toward sleep, drifting. I'm in that place where I'm not quite asleep, but not awake either, only aware enough to know I'm not asleep. Delta shifts, murmurs in her sleep, wiggles. She's snugged up against me now. I slip toward wakefulness by a few degrees, but not enough to be in any kind of control over myself. I know, in some hazy place in the back of my mind, that we're not supposed to be snuggling like this, but it feels good. It feels comfortable. It feels right. Her butt nestles perfectly against me, and my arm falls naturally over her waist. She wiggles again, shimmying her ass against me. Her hand flutters like a lost butterfly, finds mine, and rests on her hip, her palm against the back of my hand. Intimate, sweet, and comforting, and arousing all at the same time. I'm still not totally awake, just enough to know this isn't a dream, but sleepy enough to convince myself it is.

She makes a sleepy sound again, shifts again, and her hand tightens on mine. Tugs my hand so my arm is wrapped around her; the placement of my arm means my hand is cupping one of her breasts. I felt her moving around last night, as I was falling asleep, and I realize now she'd been taking her bra off. God, she's soft. Squishy, heavy in my hand. I'm helpless to fight the drift back upward into wakefulness, awareness. I want to stay in this warm, hazy in-between place, where I can pretend I'm not aware of what I'm doing, or how I'm holding her, touching her. She said last night she was afraid of herself, of what she'd do if we were this close. I get that—I'm equally worried about myself and what I might do.

I know she's right. This isn't anything real. There

never was anything except a strong mutual attraction, and a strangely intense bond created by the experience of working together as we have been. She has her life, I have mine; she's a single mother, I'm a vagabond. There's no way to reconcile the vast differences in our lives, and no reason to even try. We could sleep together, but it would be a momentary distraction and nothing more.

It can't be anything more. It's just not possible.

But *damn*, she feels good pressed against me like this. Her breast in my hand, her butt against my thighs and groin. I can't honestly say the erection I'm getting is morning wood—it's not, it's totally and completely sexual arousal, which I'm powerless to combat.

I'm awake now. My eyes are closed, and I'm trying to pretend I'm asleep, but I'm not. I'm memorizing the feel of Delta spooned against me, the soft, warm weight of her breast in my hand. When she wakes up, what will I do? What will she do?

She murmurs again, a wordless, muzzy mumble in her sleep. She shifts again, wiggles her butt, arches her back. My heart hammers as I realize she's beginning to wake up. I should move my hand. Shift away. But I don't want to. And she has a firm grip on my hand, keeping it where it is, and thus, in effect, pinning me in place. I'm reluctant as hell to move. I like the feel of her, and I don't want it to end.

Her butt shimmies again, and it does nothing to lessen the ache of my erection.

"Mmmmmm. Jonny." Her voice is a low murmur, just above a whisper. Sleepy, delicate, and musical.

I just make an *mmmm-hmmmm* noise in my throat, not trusting myself to talk. Not wanting to break the spell.

Her hand tightens on mine, then her fingers splay, thread between mine so our hands are tangled together. She slides our hands downward, to the hem of her shirt and up and under, so my palm is whispering over her bare flesh. Up and up, and then my hand is back where it was a moment ago, cupping her breast, except now it's against her bare skin. Her nipple is a hard button against the center of my palm, and her flesh isn't just warm, it's hot. We're beneath the blanket, covered from shoulders to feet, and the air is cool beyond the blanket, but our body heat has us warm as toast.

Her fingers leave mine, and her hips flex, tilting her butt against me. Intentionally, this time. There's no doubt she's writhing against me.

Dammit. This is exactly what I said was not going to happen, and it's exactly what she was worried was going to happen. And now . . .

It's happening.

I want it, and I'm not strong enough to stop it. Self-control has never been my strongest suit, especially when it comes to women, and I don't think I've ever been as attracted to a woman as I am to Delta.

And if she wants this just as much, then any chance

of stopping this before it becomes something complicated and messy is pretty much screwed.

"Delta," I whisper.

She wiggles her butt against me, and my cock throbs. "Jonny." She sighs, a soft sound of pleasure. "You feel good."

"So do you," I admit. "Too good."

"No such thing."

I groan as she begins to writhe against me rhythmically. I want to touch her. Make her feel good. I want to hear that moan again. And I absolutely fucking should not do this.

I shouldn't release the warm weight of her breast and slide my hand down her flat belly, tracing with my fingertips the seams and scars from childbirth. I shouldn't flick open the fly of her shorts or lower the zipper. No way in hell should I delve my fingers under the waistband of her underwear and into the silky thatch of closely trimmed fuzz over her core. It's a super crazy bad idea for me to trace my middle finger along the seam of her pussy and swipe that finger between the lips and into her wet channel. I shouldn't crave the way she moans so breathlessly at my touch. I really, *really* shouldn't relish, down to the fibers of my soul, the way the writhing of her hips shifts into something new, a different kind of movement, a new desperation. Fingering her wet, pulsing pussy shouldn't feel this good. Feeling her quake under my touch, feeling her start to come apart shouldn't be this amazing.

It shouldn't be the most erotic moment of my life when she grinds herself against my fingers as I circle her clit and bring her to orgasm.

But, one hundred percent truth—it is.

I was already hard as a damn rock, but when Delta spasms and whimpers, biting her lip to keep from screaming, gyrating against me, it's enough to make me start to seep pre-come.

After a few moments of quaking and whimpering, Delta lets out a long, low moan of pleasure, stilling. "God, Jonny. That was—one of the best orgasms I've ever had." She shimmies, and I feel her wiggling out of her shorts and underwear, and she's pretty much naked under the blanket. She spins in place, and her eyes meet mine. "Don't say a word, Jonny. Don't move, don't speak. Just . . . go with it, okay?"

I let out a breath as she opens my shorts. "Delta, I—"

Her finger touches my lips, shushing me. "I'm serious." She shifts my shorts and underwear down past my hips and I kick them off but leave them under the blanket with us. "Nothing has changed. I know that. But I also know I can't help it . . ." She shrugs a shoulder, keeping her eyes locked on me as she grasps my erection with one hand. "I *need* this with you, Jonny. Damn the consequences. I just . . . I need this."

She strokes me until I'm growling and groaning, then she moves astride me. Tugging the blanket over her shoulders so we're both covered, she rolls the hem of her shirt up so her breasts are bared, and she braces her weight with one hand. Grabs my cock with the other, and guides me to her entrance.

I know what she asked of me, but I can't stay silent. "Delta, are you sure? I don't have protection."

"Are you clean?"

I nod. "I get tested regularly, and I always use a condom. I usually keep some with me, but I lost everything when Christian's ship went down."

She notches me into her slit, sucking in a gasp. "I'm clean too. Promise. And I'm on the shot."

"Delta—"

"We're safe, Jonny. There's nothing else I care about." She stares down at me, eyes wide, breathing hard, drawing out the moment before I fully penetrate her. "I know I should care, and I know this is stupid, but I don't care. And I *know* you can't tell me you don't want this as much as I do."

I groan at the feel of her, just barely hugging the tip of my erection. Her bare breasts sway, the tips brushing my chest. Her eyes are so blue in the darkness, her skin is so pale, her curves so lush and tempting. God, how can I refuse this? I know, like she said, this is stupid, but she also pinpointed exactly how I feel: in this moment, I don't care.

I wrap one hand around the back of her head, and the other around her waist. I lift up and smash my mouth

against hers, and in the same moment I thrust up with my hips and tug her down onto me. I feel her slide down around my aching cock, sheathing me in her tight wet heat, and I groan into the kiss, and Delta groans with me. The kiss explodes into furious fire, our tongues clashing and tangling. She gives me her weight, collapsing onto me, hands in my hair, and her hips begin to piston.

Her lips tremble, breaking the kiss as she groans raggedly. "Jesus, Jonny. Holy shit."

Her forehead touches mine, and I release my grip on her hair so I can stroke her skin everywhere I can reach, neck and shoulders, arms, her sides and her hips and her ass and her thighs, caressing her flesh hungrily as we find our rhythm together. It's never been like this before. There's never been this kind of . . . urgency. This madness. This wild, crazed, fury. This spark blooming into flame, this flame exploding into wildfire, this wildfire coalescing into something hotter and bigger and madder than a star, than a whole host of stars. I feel alive as never before, as if before this moment I was only a zombie, trudging listlessly through life. A ship blown by only a breath of wind, but now the wind has suddenly picked up to send me scudding with dizzying speed across the waves.

I kiss her everywhere my mouth can find to kiss. I can't not kiss her, can't not touch her.

It's never been so easy to find a synchronized rhythm with a woman. We just . . . *fit*. Her hips fit against mine, her ass fits against my thighs, her big lush silky tits brush perfectly against me as she moves, her face fits into my hands and her mouth fits against my mouth, and her hands feel like perfection, burying in my hair and tangling and gripping and tugging. She just *fits* me, so perfectly.

"Delta, Delta—" I wish I knew what else to say. I want to give her poetry, but that's not me, so I moan her name as I thrust into the soaked and slippery grip of her channel. "God, Delta. *Dios mio, eres hermosa*, Delta . . . you feel so fucking good."

She shudders above me, which does delicious things to her breasts, and she slams downward, taking me deep, hard. "It makes me crazy when you speak Spanish to me." She bites the lobe of my ear then my lower lip, lifting up and crushing down with earthquaking intensity. "Say something else."

I let my mouth run away from me, in Spanish. *"Fuck, Delta, you feel like heaven. You feel so good it makes me crazy. I'm crazy about you. This is crazy. I'm crazy for doing this, but I can't help it. I don't want this to end. I want to keep fucking you forever, I want to fuck you just like this until neither of us can move."*

I feel her coming apart on top of me, shuddering, clinging to my neck with both arms, lips against my cheek, stuttering and scraping over my stubble, gasping in my ear.

"Oh God, oh God, oh God!" she chants. "Don't

stop, Jonny. I'm coming, holy shit oh my God oh shit, I'm coming so hard Jonny!"

I keep talking to her in Spanish as she comes; I almost never revert to Spanish, ever, even in the most intense situations, but now I can't help it, my lifelong command of English has just totally fled and I'm left with Spanish, and I'm unaware of what I'm saying.

"What are you doing to me? How can you make this feel so good? This is better than anything has ever felt—I want to keep going forever. Don't stop fucking me, Delta. God, don't stop, don't stop, I'm so close, Delta. I'm going to come so hard you'll fucking taste it. You'll be leaking my come for days, Delta." I grind up into her, gripping the creases of her hips in both hands now, snarling into her ear as I reach my own climax, while she's still spasming and whimpering through hers above me. "You feel it, Delta? Feel me coming? I'm coming so hard, Delta—*I'm filling you with my come, you feel it?* You feel me?"

That last part was a mix of Spanish and English, I think, but it's hard to be sure when I'm exploding so hard I can't breathe, so hard I feel like I'm pouring a portion of my actual soul into her, though the joining of our bodies.

She is shuddering and shrieking shrilly past clenched teeth. "Look at me, Jonny." My eyes snap open. "I don't know what you're saying, but it sounds sexy as hell."

She slows then, and I'm so raggedly empty that it's

hard to breathe, and Delta seems the same way. She collapses on top of me, and I'm still inside her, going soft but neither of us seem to care.

"Delta," I start.

She's nestled on my chest, her entire body on top of mine, her head tucked under my jaw, her hands feathered into my hair. She shakes her head back and forth. "Don't. Not yet. Just . . . let me enjoy this for a minute, okay?"

I sigh, because those are pretty much my thoughts exactly. I have a million thoughts running through my head, but I can't get any of them past my lips in English or Spanish, and I don't want this moment to end, so I settle for letting my hands roam Delta's body. I play with her hair, and stroke the narrow bones of her shoulder, and trace the curve of her spine, and palm the juicy bounce of her beautiful ass.

She murmurs something under her breath, which I can't quite catch.

"You say something, Delta?" I ask.

She twitches a shoulder in what feels like a shy shrug. "Not really.

"Delta."

She sighs. "I like the way you touch me, and I hate that the sun is rising already."

I glance at the horizon and see the sun is staining the horizon pink, which means our stolen moment is nearly over.

"I like touching you, and I hate that the sun is rising too."

"Can you stop it from going up any more? So we can go again?"

I laugh softly. "Used to be, I'd be ready again in a few minutes. Nowadays, it takes a little longer than it used to."

Delta's lips touch my jaw, kissing gently, then her palm presses into my cheek, turning my face so her mouth can find mine. "I don't care how long it takes, Jonny. I just want you again," she breathes, only breaking the kiss long enough to get out the words, before kissing me again. "I don't want this to end."

"Me either."

"Why does it have to?"

"Been over this."

"I know." She sighs, letting the silence stretch between us for a minute or two, before starting again, hesitant. "Was that—you and me, just now, did it feel . . .?" She trails off as if unsure how to finish the question.

"I don't have words for what it was, Delta." I shake my head and kiss her, trying to ignore the way things in the region of my chest are twisting and aching. "I wish things were different."

"Me too." She shifts on me, and I feel her clenching around me. "I know, I know—you have to go. And I have to go be with my sister. My son needs me. A hundred reasons why this cannot go on. Doesn't make me want

you any less, though. Crazy as it is, stupid as it is, I just
. . . I fucking *want* you, Jonny Nuñez. And no matter
what happens, I'm glad we had this."

Dammit, dammit, dammit.

"Me too, Delta Martin."

Not sure how long we lie there in our little nest in
the sand, the sun rising in shifting washes of pink to red
to gold, the ocean shushing us, the gulls trying in vain to
rouse us. I feel her heart beating; I feel her hands clutching my hair with desperation; I feel her core pulsing
around me, her muscles clenching and releasing; she's
clutching me on purpose, I think. Trying to arouse me.

It's working, damn her.

She feels it, feels me hardening inside her. She nuz-
zles her lips and nose and forehead into the side of my
throat, kissing and kissing and kissing, so softly, so sweet-
ly that my heart clenches and my head spins and my soul
aches for an hour more, a day more, a week more with
her.

"Delta," I breathe.

"Sssshhhhhh."

"I'm not trying to stop this, I just—"

"You can't stop this. It's already happening. Just hush,
Jonny. Just . . . hush."

Delta's hands close around my face, her palms on
my cheeks, her thumbs brushing my cheekbones, her
fingertips playing with my earlobes and the stubble on
my jaw, and she's kissing me fiercely, deeply, sucking my

breath from me then giving me her breath and slashing at my tongue with hers, and I'm so hard now it hurts, aches, throbs. I'm inside her, Delta's tight channel is spasming around me, wet and hot and intoxicatingly perfect. She moves then. Holding my face. Kissing me. I have both hands in her hair, and I'm kissing her back and moving with her and moaning, muttering I don't even know what in Spanish.

I have to . . . I have to take her how I want her. How I've envisioned taking her, since the moment I met her.

I roll, putting her beneath me. I adjust the blanket so we're still both covered, and I brace my hands in the sand by her face and I lean down and I kiss her mouth, and then I slide my mouth down her soft pale skin to her breasts, and I devour them greedily. I suck her nipple into my mouth and flick it with my tongue until she's mewling helplessly, and I'm moving into her, thrusting slowly, lazily.

She clings to me, her hands on my butt, pulling at me, encouraging me, silently begging me to go faster, harder. I resist, taking my time. I graze my mouth across the valley between her tits and kiss and lick and suckle the other nipple. Back and forth, using my hands on one breast while my mouth is occupied on the other. Her legs curl around mine, and she's whimpering quietly.

She shudders, and her hand steals between our bodies. Delta fingers herself as I thrust into her, bringing herself swiftly to orgasm with a few economical circles of her fingers, and I feel her channel tighten and spasm around me, and her teeth nip at my neck, and her breath huffs hot on my ear; the feel of her coming around my cock takes me to the edge.

Delta's eyes search and find mine. She pulls at my ass, wraps her legs higher around mine, urging me. "Come with me, Jonny!" she whispers fiercely, desperately. "Come with me! God, I'm coming so hard, Jonny, and I want to feel you come too."

I let go. Fuck her with urgency, growling as I reach my own orgasm, and Delta is still coming, or coming again, I'm not sure which. Doesn't matter, because she's gasping frantically and smashing her hips against mine, and I release with a low, guttural growl.

"Delta, Delta . . ." I bite out her name in a chant, and I've reverted to Spanish yet again, something only she seems able to make me do. *"Take it, Delta. Take it all. Do you feel me coming inside you? You feel so fucking good I can't handle it. Too good. You feel too good. God, Delta, don't stop, don't stop!"*

We move in perfect unison, thrusting in synch, groaning together, coming simultaneously, kissing raggedly and breathing harshly and gasping together and moving with furious desperation together until we're both spent and breathless. I let her have my weight, and she takes it eagerly, stroking my hair and caressing my back and my butt and my arms: everywhere. Breathing with me. Whispering my name as we catch our breath.

"My fucking God, Jonny," she says, finally. "What *was* that?"

I shake my head. "I don't know. I don't know, Delta."

"It's fucking crazy what you make me feel, Jonny."

"I know." I roll off her, and she rolls with me, immediately returning to settle into the nook of my arm. "I feel it, too, Delta. Don't think I don't."

Dawn is in full effect, now. We lie together in contented silence for a while, and I'm even starting to drift off again when Delta lets out a muffled giggle.

"What's funny?" I ask.

She giggles again. "I'm leaking." A pause, and I feel her shifting her legs, sliding them together. "Like, a *lot*."

"Um. Sorry?"

She shook her head. "Don't be. I just didn't think about this particular aspect of this."

"Me either."

She wiggles again, laughing. "Eww. Every time I move more come squishes out of me."

"You could rinse off in the ocean," I suggest. "Might be a bit brisk, but . . . you'd be clean."

"Clean . . . *er*, maybe." She lifts up to look at me. "Are you suggesting we go skinny dipping in the ocean right now?"

"You, not me. I don't have come leaking out of me."

"Well, not anymore. And I wouldn't call it a leak, exactly." She snickers. "More of a howitzer sort of situation, judging by the amount of come I've got leaking out of me."

I can't help laughing. "I feel like I should apologize for making you messy, but I also feel weirdly proud, too."

She smacks me on the chest. "Proud? You feel proud of filling me to the brim with your sperm?"

I shrug. "Yeah, kind of."

"It's gross!" she protests.

I lift up on an elbow so I'm over her, staring down at her. "You like it."

She blinks at me. "Do not."

I gaze back steadily. "Yes, you do. Admit it. You *like* being full of my come. You want more of it."

She sighs heavily, and her face twists. "I do. I really, really do. I like it. No—I *love* it, and yeah, I want more of it." She seems to give in to sadness for a moment then wiggles out from underneath me to sit up, tossing the blanket off of us; glancing around to determine that we're still alone, she shrugs out of her shirt, tosses it at my face, and laughs. "Last one in is a rotten egg!"

And then she's gone, tearing off across the beach toward the water. I bolt after her, feet digging into the sand. She's fast, but I'm faster. I reach her moments before she reaches the water, grab her around the waist, haul her into the water, throw her bodily, and dive after her. She splashes into the waves, squealing, and I'm right there with her as she surfaces, spluttering and laughing.

"Asshole," she says, laughing. "I was going in by myself."

"Yeah, but that was more fun."

"Fuck, it's cold."

"I thought you grew up here?"

"Other side, Gulf side. It's a little warmer." We're waist deep but crouched so we're fully immersed. Delta stands up, dripping, and her nipples are hard and she's so beautiful it hurts. "You're looking at me funny, Jonny."

I stand to face her, slip my hands around her waist and pull her close, and she wraps her arms around my shoulders. "Just looking at you. Admiring you." I kiss her, and we move deeper into the cold waves. *"You are so fucking beautiful,"* I say in Spanish.

"What's that mean?" Delta asks. I tell her, and she ducks her head, laughing sarcastically. "You're only saying that because we just fucked twice."

I shake my head. "No, Delta. I'm not. I'm saying it because it's true."

She swallows hard, pulls away from me, dives into the water, and swims a couple feet away, then crouches in the surf, scrubbing at her armpits and between her legs. "You can't say shit like that, Jonny."

"Why not?"

"Because I'll start to believe you actually mean it."

"So? I *do* mean it."

She shakes her head again. "It's better for both of us, I think, if you're just flattering me because we had good sex."

I try to wrap my head around that and fail. "Not sure

what you mean by that. I wouldn't flatter you *after* sex, if you were trying to think negatively of me. I'd flatter you *before*, so you'd fuck me, and then stop acting like I care. If I'm flattering you after sex, it stands to reason I really mean it." I frown at her. "And why would it be better for either of us for you to think the worst of me?"

She doesn't answer right away. After scrubbing herself, she rolls onto her back and heads into the oncoming waves. She floats, her breasts just barely peeking above the water. "Because . . . because I'm a clinger, and I'm trying not to let myself go there, but you're making it really fucking difficult, okay?"

"A clinger? What do you mean, you're a clinger?"

She stops swimming and moves so she's standing with the water just above her breasts and shakes her head again. Not a denial so much as a . . . an expression of not knowing what to say, I think.

"I get clingy. Emotionally attached quickly."

"Oh."

She nods. "Yep. Oh. Not so beautiful anymore, huh? Nobody likes a clinger, especially when she's a single mom nearing forty."

"Delta, it's not like that."

"Exactly."

I shake my head and swim toward her. "You're misunderstanding me, Delta. When I say it's not like that, I mean I'm disagreeing with what you said about yourself. You and me not being able to . . . I don't know . . .

be together, I guess—it's not about you being a single mother, or clingy, and I'm over forty myself."

Delta sighs and swims backward away from me. "Jonny, goddammit. You're not helping."

"What? You *want* me to be an asshole?"

She laughs. "Yes, actually. I mean, no. But yes."

"Well, that's clear as mud."

"It would be easier for me to walk away if you were an asshole. But obviously, you're not an asshole, thus making it all the more difficult."

I don't know what to say to that. "Delta—"

She waves a hand to stop me. "Don't, Jonny. It's gonna suck. It is what it is." She glances past me at the shore. "Better get out while the getting is good. People are gonna be up soon."

She swims past me, staying low in the water until she has to climb out and trot ashore. I stay in the water and watch, because *damn*, the woman is beautiful. The way her body moves, the way the right things bounce just the right way when she jogs ashore? Takes all my willpower to stay here in the water. I have to, though. If I go ashore with her, I'll only make things worse.

I want her.

I don't want to let go.

I shouldn't have slept with her. I shouldn't have. Now I have the taste of her on my lips, and the feel of her skin on my hands, and the scent of her on me, and the memory of the way she felt. I don't regret it, not in the slightest, but when I do finally leave, it's going to hurt.

Delta wipes her body dry with the blanket, slinks into her clothes, and bends forward to wring out her hair. I just watch. I'm frozen, my bones aching in the cold Atlantic water. I don't follow her, I accept the cold. I want to touch her again. Hold her again. Make her scream. Take her somewhere private and do things right, not just a stolen few moments on a beach.

I stay where I am until she's gone. When she's out of sight, I emerge from the ocean and use the blanket, like she did, to dry off somewhat, and dress, and plan my next move.

It's time to visit Ava and discharge my duty as Christian's best friend.

5

After getting dressed and leaving the beach, I go in search of coffee. I don't have to go far, as there's an enterprising individual with a push-cart containing a gas camping stove, a kettle, bottled water, and a drip coffee setup. I gladly pay the five bucks per cup, since there's not a coffee shop or restaurant open anywhere nearby. I buy two coffees, wait a good ten minutes for them to be prepared, and take them back toward the nest Jonny and I have been sharing over the last few days.

He's dressed, his hair is wet and messy, and he's gathering up his things. I sit on the edge of the boardwalk watching him. He notices me and the coffee, which I hand to him.

"Thanks," he says.

I just smile, watching him wrap the last of his supplies into the blanket, which he sets near me on the boardwalk. Then he hops up to sit beside me, the metal box tucked under his arm.

We sip coffee together in silence.

He finally eyes me. "What's your plan?"

I shrug. "I don't know. I might try to get Ava to come back to Chicago with me and Alex."

"Probably be good for her not to be alone right now, I think."

I glance at Jonny. "You think he's dead? Christian, I mean?"

He shrugs. "I don't know. With my experience and my knowledge of the odds given the situation, I'd say, yeah, there's literally no chance he could have made it. But . . . as his best friend? I want to believe he found a way to survive."

"What are you going to do?"

He blows out a breath. "I don't know. The ship I came in on has a spot for me. Dominic is a good man, a good captain. It's not a sailing job, but after my journey with Chris . . . I'm not sure I want to sail again right away. I might go with Dominic and do some trawling for a while."

"Who is Dominic?"

"Dominic Bathory. Owns a deep-sea trawler. Picked me off *The Hemingway* after the storm, stitched up my leg, brought me here." He waves up the coast. "He's north of here a ways, helping with the offshore clean-up. The plan was for me to find Ava, give her the box and make sure she was in an okay place, and then join Dominic on the boat."

"So what changed?" I ask.

He doesn't answer for a while, sipping his coffee. "I dunno. Nothing, I guess." He glances at me. "And everything."

"Everything, meaning what?"

"Everything, meaning you."

I let out a breath. "Oh." I shake my head. "That doesn't change anything, though, does it?"

He groans. "Delta, I don't—"

I hold up a hand to stall him. "I'm not asking anything of you, Jonny. We've talked about this already. Nothing has changed. You sail, and I'm raising a kid. Ft. Lauderdale isn't my home; Chicago is. So it's not like if I was to say you could visit me . . ." I trail off, shaking my head. "Never mind." I smile at him again. "It was a good thing while it lasted, Jonny."

"Yeah, it was." He glances at the sun, now fully risen over the horizon. "About time to go see Ava."

"That's what I'm thinking." I stand up, coffee in hand. "Ready?"

He eyes the blanket full of things. Glances up the boardwalk, sees a man who was clearly homeless before the hurricane and is in more dire straits after it; the homeless man is dressed in rags, feet clad in shoes that are little more than shreds, carrying a plastic garbage bag full of who knows what. Jonny grabs the makeshift sack of supplies wrapped in the blanket and carries it to the man. They exchange a few words, and the homeless man can be heard effusively thanking Jonny, who just nods and waves and walks back to me.

"Now I'm ready," Jonny says.

I glance at him as we walk in the direction of the hospital. "Why'd you give him that stuff? Don't you need it?"

He shrugs and shakes his head. "Nah. I can make do, find what I need, plus I'll be aboard *The Glory of Gloucester* soon anyway."

I laugh. "The what?"

Jonny chuckles. "Dominic's boat, *The Glory of Gloucester*. It's a joke, I think. He's from Gloucester, Massachusetts. I dunno why he named it that, but it feels like a joke, since as far as deep-sea trawlers go, he'd agree she's no glory of anything. Seaworthy, clean, tidy, well kept, and dependable—which is all you can ask of a ship, in my opinion—but she's not a glorious craft by any stretch of anyone's imagination."

"Well, it was nice of you to give that stuff to that guy."

Jonny waves a hand. "Don't make it out to be too altruistic or nothing. Mainly, I didn't want to carry it around with me."

We follow the beach and the boardwalk for several

blocks, chatting easily. We're maybe another five-minute walk away from the hospital when Jonny asks me a question that leaves me reeling.

"So, Delta. Tell me about Alex."

"Um." I blink, and have to think, because I'm not used to talking about my son with men I've slept with. "Well. He's six. He has my eyes, but in every other way he looks just like his sperm donor. Which, honestly, isn't a bad thing, since he was a hell of a good-looking guy, but he's a rich douchebag who doesn't give a shit about anyone. Alex has Tom's blond hair, his perfect facial structure, and his charm, but he has my eyes, my chin, and my . . . um . . . feistiness.

"So Alex is feisty and takes no shit, but he's charming as hell about it. It's a problem, honestly. I tell him no, like no, Alex, you can't have ice cream for breakfast, and I'll turn around and he's eating ice cream anyway. I'll start yelling at him, and he'll yell back, and I'll get mad, and then right when my head is about to fucking explode, he comes over and gives me a big hug and a big kiss and snuggles me and bats those stupid thick eyelashes of his and tells me he's so sorry, he just couldn't help it, and can I please forgive him. And what am I supposed to do? He's being so sweet and so genuine; I can't be angry anymore."

Jonny laughs. "Sounds like a little player in the making, if you ask me."

I groan. "Seriously, don't even remind me. He already

has all the women in his school wrapped around his little finger, teachers, the principal and lunch ladies included." I glance at him. "Why do you ask about Alex?"

He shrugs. "Just curious, I guess. He's your kid, and he's an important part of your life, so I figure if I know something about him, I'll know something about you."

"I thought we weren't doing this."

"I'm not doing anything. Just making conversation."

"I don't typically talk about Alex with men. It's a little weird for me, honestly."

"Why?"

I frown at him as we approach the entrance to the hospital, which is swarming with people coming in and going out. "Why what? Why don't I talk about him, or why is it weird?"

Jonny shrugs. "Yes?"

"I don't talk about him because most men aren't interested in hearing about him. They're only interested in me for as long as it seems likely I'll put out for them. Once they find out about Alex, *poof*, they're gone. And if they do express interest, it's just to seem like they're not only interested in me for sex, but it's all fake—they don't really give a shit, and I wouldn't take them around him anyway.

"I know better than to think any man will actually be interested in me *and* Alex, as a unit. That's too much commitment for the men I've come across. So I use the men for sex like they use me, and I don't talk about Alex, ever, and that's that. I can't believe I'm saying all this, Jonny, it's kind of like a magician revealing her secrets, only I'm not a magician, just a trashy almost-forty single mother, a washed-up, has-been, never-was, wannabe singer-songwriter.

"So talking about Alex is weird, because . . . I don't know. It's not like he's a secret, he's just a part of my life I try to keep totally separate from my need for sex."

"I'm not the type to pretend like I care about something, Delta, so don't think that's why I'm asking."

I laugh. "Again, like before, that's what's confusing me. My instinct is to assume the worst because that's what I'm used to, only I can't do that with you because you're showing me these sensitive, considerate parts of yourself *after* we fucked. Which obviously makes it *not* about you trying to get into my pants, since you've already done that. We've also agreed there's nothing possible between us besides what we did, so why bother? It doesn't make any sense."

He shrugs. "I have no answers, Delta."

I laugh again. "Yeah, well . . . maybe try to be a little more douchey, okay? So I can walk away with at least *some* of my heart intact, otherwise I'll always be wondering what could have been between us, if circumstances were different."

He shakes his head, chuckling. "Yeah, I'll work on that."

"Thanks. Besides, nobody likes a sensitive guy, don't

you know that? Douchey assholes get all the action."

He gives me a look that's equal parts frown of disap-
proval and smirk of amusement. "Nice guys finish last,
huh?"

I smirk back. "Nice guys don't usually *finish* at all,
because they're not getting any to begin with."

"Yeah, well, I finished twice, and I like to think I'm at
least *kind of* nice." He quirks an eyebrow at me.

I sigh. "You are clearly an exception to the rule. And
anyway, what if I only fucked you for your looks?"

He laughs outright. "I've never been accused of being handsome, Delta. Maybe I'm not exactly ugly, but
I'm no Antonio Banderas."

By now we're up on Ava's floor, dodging nurses and
doctors and orderlies as they scurry about the hallways.
There are patients in beds in the hallways, and as we pass
a waiting room, family members are asleep on couches,
a doctor's curled up in a ball on the floor in one corner,
and two nurses are leaning against each other, sitting up
with their backs to the wall, fast asleep. This hospital
is clearly way, way over capacity, and way, way under-
staffed, but everyone is doing what they can, and then
some.

I bump Jonny with my shoulder. "You're sexier than
you'll ever know, Jonny."

He shakes his head. "You need glasses, babe."

"Self-deprecation doesn't fit you," I say. "Bring back
cocky Jonny."

"Oh, I'm plenty cocky, all right," he says, smirking at me. "It's all about attitude and presentation. I learned that a long time ago."

We reach Ava's room and notice one of the beds is gone, leaving only three people to the room. Ava is on the far side, against the window, so we have to skirt past the ends of the first two beds to reach hers. She's sitting up, staring out the window. The devastation is clearly visible from her window: condos and buildings damaged, streets flooded, cars abandoned and overturned, debris everywhere. She sees me enter, and her face brightens.

"Delta!" She shifts in the bed, extending her arms to me as I draw near, rounding the bed to sit on the window side. "Oh my God, I'm going crazy—you have to get me out of here!"

"That's the plan, little sis," I say.

Ava sees Jonny, and her smile fades. "Hi, Jonny."

He has the box in his hands, and he perches on the edge of the bed, opposite me. "I have something for you."

She eyes the box, shaking her head. "No. I don't want it."

He sighs deeply, wincing. "I know, Ava. I'm sorry. But . . . I swore to Chris I'd give it to you, if anything happened."

Tears slip down her cheeks, and she shakes her head. "Nothing has happened. He's out there. He's okay. I can feel him."

Jonny is visibly struggling. "I want to believe that, too. But the search and rescue crews searched several thousand square miles of ocean and found nothing. The only reason I was found was blind luck." He reaches for her hand, but she jerks it out of his reach. "He was my best friend, Ava. He was like a younger brother to me."

Ava blinks fiercely. "Stop saying *was*, Jonny. He's *alive*, okay? He's out there. I *know* he is."

"If anyone could survive what happened, it's Chris. He's smart, he's tough—he's a survivor. I feel it too, okay? I do. I swear I do. But if he is alive, he could be anywhere. I was found hundreds of miles away from where we were when the storm hit, and if he is alive, it's because he was picked up by someone. He could be literally anywhere in the world."

Ava shakes her head. "He'll find me. He'll come home."

I hate having to deliver another piece of bad news. "Ava, sweetheart. There's nothing left of your condo. The building is . . . it has to be totally demolished."

She shakes her head again. "Then I'll buy a new one. I have to be here when he comes home. I *have* to." She stares out the window. "I'm not leaving, Delta. When he comes looking for me, he'll come here. He'd . . . he'll know I wouldn't leave until he came home."

"There's no home left, Ava. The city is . . . it's going to be months at least before anything is remotely liveable again." I take her hand, and she lets me. "I'm here for you, Ava. No matter what. I think you have to hope for the best but prepare for the worst, okay? Just be realistic. This whole area of the coast is wiped out. I want you to come to St. Pete's with me. You don't have to stay with Mom and Dad, obviously, since you can probably afford your own place. But you'd be around family. Somewhere that's safe, until you can get back on your feet."

She stares hard at me. "We both left home for a reason, Delta. I'm not going back to St. Pete's."

"Then come to Chicago with me. Chris knows I live in Chicago, and it's not like there's that many Delta Martins in the phone book. I'm not hard to find."

"No!" Ava shifts, trying to get away from me, but in the process catches up against Jonny. "You shouldn't have come. You're overwhelming me."

"You have to figure this out, Ava," I say. "You can't stay here much longer. They need the bed, and you're going crazy, you said so yourself. You're healthy now, and you have to figure out what you're going to do. I know you . . . I know you miss Chris, and I hope he's alive, too. But you can't . . . you can't pretend nothing happened."

Her eyes water, and tears trickle freely. "I know something happened, Delta. Fucking *everything* happened. We lost baby Henry, and then Chris left me, and . . . and . . . and then the storm, and I know he's out there somewhere and he needs me, and I need him and I—I can't leave, I can't, Delta. I just *can't*."

"There's nothing here, Ava," I say. "I've been out there and so has Jonny. It's a mess, a total disaster. There's nowhere to go. If you don't want to go to St. Pete's, and you don't want to go to Chicago, the maybe we can . . . I don't know . . . get a place together in Miami or something. I think they missed the worst of it. I just . . . I don't want you to be alone."

"I *won't* be alone," Ava snaps. "Christian will find me."

"And I'll be with you until then."

She obviously doesn't want to be alone, since she hesitates, considering what I'm saying. "I can't ask you to move Alex."

"He's a resilient kid. He'll be fine. He loves you, and living with Auntie Ava would be fun for him. He sounds like he's having the time of his life with Mom and Dad, too. They're probably spoiling him rotten."

"That'd be a first," Ava mutters.

"I know. But it seems to be good for Alex, so whatever." I sigh. "Maybe they'll be better grandparents than they were parents."

"Yeah, maybe," Ava says, not sounding convinced.

"I wasn't crazy about leaving him with them at first, but when I heard about the hurricane, I obviously couldn't bring him with me, so I didn't have many options." I pause, glance at Jonny, then back at Ava. "I think you should hear what Jonny has to say, Ava."

She shakes her head. "I don't want to," she whispers.

"It'll be admitting he's gone."

"No, Ava," Jonny says. "This box just contains letters and stuff. I don't know for sure since I haven't opened it. I only know it was important to him. He made me promise to bring it to you."

She takes the box. "Fine. Thank you for bringing it."

Jonny reaches inside his shirt and pulls out the thin gold chain he never takes off. He unclasps it, unstrings a small brass key from the chain, re-clasps the chain and crucifix around his neck, and hands the key to Ava. "You'll need this to open it."

Ava takes the key, holds the box on her lap, and stares at the key. "How did you make it out of the storm, Jonny? What—what happened?"

Jonny is silent a long while, staring out the window, and I think he's seeing the storm rather than Ft. Lauderdale. "It blew up out of nowhere and hit us like a goddamn Mack truck." He glances at Ava, gazes at her with an intense expression on his face. "We'd rounded the Horn and were getting ready to head into the Indian Ocean. I think Chris was planning on stopping at Madagascar for a while, maybe. I dunno. We were in Port Elizabeth. We'd taken on supplies, spent some time after rounding the Horn, kicking it on the mainland. This was . . . March? There was some stuff that happened around Valentine's Day, and it ended up being just Chris and me again."

Ava frowns. "The French girl. Marty or something."

Jonny nods. "Yeah. Marta. Great sailor, good woman. Messed up in the head, like both Chris and me, so it worked out pretty well for a while."

"A good woman, huh?" She sounds . . . skeptical. "What happened on Valentine's Day, Jonny?"

Jonny shrugs. "Not my story to tell. Marta left a couple weeks after that, though."

"Did Christian tell you what happened?"

"*Jesus Cristo*," Jonny mutters. "Sort of, but not really. In a vague sort of way . . . but, like I said, it's not my story to tell. It's Chris's, and Marta's, for that matter."

"Can you at least tell me if he slept with her?" Ava asks.

"He did not sleep with Marta."

Ava breathes out a sigh of relief and glances at Jonny again. "The storm."

"Well, after we left Port Elizabeth it was just him and me again. Marta left us there—I think she was planning on going back to France. Anyway, things weren't . . . they weren't good for Chris. He was really struggling with everything. He loved you, you know? He—he *loves* you. Still does. But everything that happened just . . . it fucked him up, you know? He was tryin' hard to sort his shit out. It wasn't easy, but he was trying.

"When he couldn't get hold of you I think he freaked out. Made him panic, a little. I know he was wondering what happened to you, realizing that whatever may have happened, he loved you and wanted to be with you. He had to see you." Jonny pauses a minute, thinking.

"I remember the conversation. I had just gotten back from a bender, and he springs all this on me, how he misses you and your email and phone and that all of those things are shut off. He told me he needs to figure things out with you. So he was like, 'I gotta go back, Jonny.'

"I never have anywhere I have to go, or anywhere I have to be, so I said: 'Chris, amigo, wherever you go, I'll go.' So we went back around the Horn and started heading west, this way. Then the storm blew up outta nowhere, smacked the shit out of us."

Jonny pauses, remembering what happened next.

"Started out like not much more than a nasty storm, but it kept getting worse. By the time we realized how bad it was going to be, there wasn't shit we could do. Never was anything to do, really. We were out on the open ocean, crossing the middle of the Atlantic. Once a storm blows up on you out in the open like that, there ain't shit to do but try to ride it out. So we rode it out. We hoisted the storm sail, reefed the sail, and did everything there was to do. The waves . . . Ava, you don't even know, *amiga*. They were huge. I been sailing my whole life, and I don't know if I've ever seen waves like that. It was bad, so bad. You go up and up and up and up, and then for a second the whole ocean is beneath you, but it's all fifty-foot waves everywhere you look, in every direction, just the black sky and the waves. They're like mountains, man, so huge you can't picture it unless you've seen it. Makes you feel tiny and powerless. You just . . . you realize you ain't shit, when you see waves like that. All you can do is hold on and fuckin' hope."

He pauses again, and he's starting to struggle with the telling. "Chris was at the wheel. Taking us up to the crests and then back down the troughs, like a fuckin' rollercoaster. We went up this one wave, had to be . . . *mierda*, I don't know—sixty, maybe seventy feet high. It picked us up, lifted us into to the sky like we were a little toy. Tossed us and we were fuckin' airborne. We hit the bottom *hard*. I heard something snap or crunch, and that was the beginning of the end.

That wave just . . . We hit the bottom, and Chris was ready for it, holding on and braced for the impact, but he was . . . thrown clear. He must have flown a good hundred feet before he hit the water. I tried to get to the wheel and turn the ship around so I could grab him. I tried to throw a ring to him, but he was under the water and then he popped up a few hundred feet away, riding a different wave, just trying to keep his head above water. He was out of sight before I could—before I could do a damn thing. I tried, Ava, I swear I tried. But he just disappeared. And the boat started listing and taking on water, and it capsized. Staying alive myself was all I could do, and I—I remember thinking I probably wasn't gonna make it out. When I woke up on Dominic's boat, I was honestly surprised to be alive."

"And this box?" Ava asks, toying with the key.

Jonny shrugs. "Last thing Chris and I talked about, like a serious talk, not just shootin' the shit, was you. He made me promise if anything happened I'd bring you the box and give it to you. It was for safekeeping, a back-up plan, just in case, you know? So when the storm hit, I made sure it was locked down and stowed away safe. And when I realized she was going down, I got the box out and held on to it for dear life. *The Hemingway* began to sink, and I ended up riding the underside of the hull for a while, but I never let go of that damn box, because Chris is my brother, and I keep my damn promises."

Ava blinks hard, keeping tears at bay. "You held on to that box while the ship went down under you? So you could bring it to me?"

He shrugs. "Yeah, like I said, I keep my promises."

I feel compelled to point something else out. "Once Jonny arrived in Ft. Lauderdale he spent three days digging through the rubble, looking for you. He pulled you out of the wreckage with his own two hands."

Ava can't keep the tears back anymore. "Th-thank you, Jonny. I guess I owe you my life."

"You don't owe me shit. I'm just sorry I couldn't get to you sooner, and I'm sorry I couldn't keep Chris alive."

"He *is* alive," Ava says, her voice hard. "He's alive. He's out there. I know he is."

"I sure as fuck hope so," Jonny says.

There's a long, long silence then, as Ava toys with

the key, staring at the box. Finally she inserts the key into the lock and twists, lifting the lid open.

I move to stand up. "You probably want some privacy, huh?"

She grabs my wrist, shaking her head as she lifts out a triple-folded piece of printer paper. "No. I—I don't want to be alone. I've been alone for so long."

"We'll stay." I glance at Jonny, and he just nods.

Ava doesn't miss the eye contact between Jonny and me, and I see a flicker of something cross her face, but she opens the first piece of paper and starts to read.

Instead of what I was expecting—more tears—Ava laughs. "Oh, Christian. You're such a melodramatic idiot." She sets the letter face down on her lap, laughter quieting into sadness. She glances at me and hands me the letter. "Will you read them to me? If I read them, I'll hear them in his voice in my head, and—I can't—I don't think I can handle that yet."

I peruse the first few paragraphs and laugh at the dramatic way he wrote. "Melodramatic idiot is right. Good grief. I've never read his novels, you know . . . are they all like this?"

Ava shakes her head. "No, not at all. Same sense of . . . fanciness, I guess you could say, but in the letter he was writing for himself, and for me, so he gave in to temptation a little. He's always tended to be . . . flowery in his writing, but he tones it back for his audience. Makes him more *accessible*, he says." She eyes me.

"You should read his books, Delta. He's a wonderful novelist."

I smile. "Maybe I will someday, when I have time to read for pleasure."

I smooth the letter against my thigh and start to read. "'*Ava, I have no intention of sending this to you. It is more of a diary or journal entry than anything else, but addressing it to you makes it easier to be honest, since I am, as you may no doubt be aware, rather facile at lying to myself, whereas I could never lie to you. Thus, I am beginning an epistolary journey . . .*'" I pause, laughing. "Jesus, what does that even mean, an epistolary journey?"

"It means—" Ava starts.

"I *know* what it means," I interrupt, feeling a little snarky, "I may not have gone to college like *some* people, but I'm not totally stupid. It was a joke."

Ava just rolls her eyes, thankfully not taking me seriously. "Oh shut up. It's not like I've rubbed the fact that I went to college in your face. And it's not like I'm any more successful than you are."

"You drive a Mercedes-Benz," I pointed out.

"Only because my *husband* is successful. I wrote one mediocre book, which sold a mediocre number of copies, and I write a mediocre blog with a mediocre number of followers." She waves a hand. "Christian is the truly talented one."

"You're still better off than I am."

Ava frowns at me. "Delta. You sold songs to four

different major country stars, three of which hit the top one hundred, and the fourth hit top ten. That's nothing to dismiss."

"Yeah, sure. And that got me precisely nowhere. I had a moment of hope, but it fizzled out like a candle in a rainstorm. I barely made enough to buy the car I'm still driving, which is now a piece of shit, because that was almost fifteen years ago."

I feel Jonny's speculative gaze on me. "You sold songs to country music stars?" he asks.

I shrug and roll my eyes. "Yeah, but that was a long time ago, and I was a whole different Delta back then."

"Didn't sound like a whole different Delta to me last night when you were singing with those people on the beach."

Ava is intensely interested. "Am I missing something?"

I wave a hand. "There were some people jamming by a bonfire, and I sang a little. No big deal." I let out a sigh. "Now, can we get back to this epistolary journey thing?" I ask, rattling the paper in my hand.

But Ava was not letting this go. "I didn't mean the singing, although that's great, and I've always said you're too talented to be stuck waitressing, but you and Jonny—"

I interrupt her by reading the letter, loudly, to shut her up before I had to answer any awkward questions. "'*Thus, I am beginning an epistolary journey, in which I*

attempt to discover myself. Revive myself. Syntactical cardio-
pulmonary resuscitation. Prosodic self-diagnosis and -medi-
cation.'" I pause with a huff.

"Prosodic self-diagnosis and -medication. Seriously?
Where does he come up with this shit?" I continue,
more seriously. *"'I've journaled most of my life, and I*
brought those notebooks with me on this trip, and I read the
backlog of journals on this computer's hard drive. I read
through them all, and I don't really like what I have read, for
the most part. I tell only one side of things. I indulge in what
you, my love, call my purple prose . . .'"

I read the rest of the letter without any additional
commentary, and, indeed, Christian truly does have a
compelling way with words, even if he does tend to be
a little over-the-top sometimes. Some parts were a little difficult to read, clearly meant solely for himself and
Ava—I felt as if I were eavesdropping on a private, intimate moment—*the warm huff of your breath on my skin*
and the wet suck of your mouth around me and the building
pressure of need reaching release. Ava, I need the sweet cream
of your cunt—I mean, Jesus.

Even I have to admit that shit is *hot*. It's not meant
for me though, it's meant for Ava. I can tell even with
my voice as a filter, she's hearing Christian. Hearing him
whisper the words to her. Whisper her name in her ear
as they fuck in the darkness.

I shiver, because it's an erotic image, even if it is my
younger sister.

But then he writes things like the last few sentences—*I loathe each of the thousands of miles between us, but I
cannot wish them away, for I hope at the end of my journey I
shall find you. Or rather, find myself, and thus . . . you. Myself
and us. I am taking the long way home, Ava*—and my heart
twists in my chest because, holy hell, that's the most romantic thing I've ever heard.

The man loved her, that much is completely evident.

I finish the letter, and Ava wordlessly hands me the
next one.

I read it through, and that one is . . . very, *very* uncomfortable for me to read. But it's so damn compelling.
It reveals so much of the man, so much I could never
have begun to understand about him had I not read that
letter. Ava is clearly emotional now, but when I finish the
second letter, she hands me the third, which is a much
thicker stack of papers. I shuffle through them, and I'm
thankful Christian numbered the pages.

"Jesus, this one is an actual fictional story, I think.
Like, a full short story." I glance at Ava. "Are you all right?
You need a break?"

She shakes her head. "No, I'm not all right, but I
don't want a break. I want to hear what he wrote."

I suck in a breath and hold it. I glance over at Jonny.
He's struggling with this, too. Missing Chris and probably feeling like an intruder on a private moment, as I am.

I read the story, "The Selkie and the Sea" and, by
the end, I'm hooked into it, fascinated by it. And when I

finish, all three of us are silent, lost in our own thoughts.

"That's really amazing," I say. "You're not kidding, Ava; he really is a talented writer."

Jonny shifts on the bed. "I never went to school, so I was barely literate, even in Spanish" he says, seemingly apropos of nothing. "I learned to speak some English as a kid because everyone learned to speak a little, but when a hurricane hit and I lost everyone, I found a spot on a freighter, working in the galley. One of the guys on that ship taught me to read and write in Spanish and then in English. So, I can read and write fluently in both Spanish and English, but . . . I'm not, like, on *that* kind of level." He reaches across Ava and taps the sheaf of paper in my hand. "So, I gotta confess, I don't really understand why he included that story in the letters he wrote you. I mean the others, I understand. But that one, I don't get."

Ava takes the story from me and flips through the pages herself for a while, rereading here and there. Eventually she sighs and glances at Jonny. "It's . . . it's a metaphor, sort of."

"A metaphor . . ." Jonny murmurs, "That's a comparison of some kind, right?"

She nods. "Right. If you were to say the sky *is* a blue blanket, that's a metaphor. If you say the waves are *like* a rollercoaster, that's a simile. Same thing, but a simile uses the words 'like' or 'as' to make the comparison." She taps the story. "This is an extended metaphor. The idea behind it is that the main character in the story, Murtagh, the selkie . . . that's Christian. When we first met in college, he was living on this tiny little sailboat in the bay, and he drove this old truck he'd fixed up. I thought it was this cute thing he did, living on the sailboat. I didn't realize then how he felt about the sea. I mean, he talked about the places he'd been, all these amazing, exotic places, and it made him seem so romantic and worldly, you know?

"But the more serious we got, the more I realized he really was living on that boat because that's where he felt most at home: on a boat. It made me nervous. Like, what if I woke up one day and his boat was gone? I knew I loved him by that point, but . . . I *hate* sailing. Delta and I grew up in St. Pete's, so I grew up on the ocean. I've been deep-sea fishing, and I like going on short boat rides and jet skiing and all that, but I like going back to dry land when I'm done. I like being in control, having a motor, knowing I can point it back toward land and go home. Sailing, being out in the open ocean . . . I don't know. It makes me feel . . . vulnerable, I guess. Unsafe."

"Part of the lure," Jonny says. "The risk, the doubt, the challenge. It's you and your boat against the whole ocean, and you have to know her and work with her and understand her and love her and even hate her, if you're gonna live out there."

Ava laughs. "You sound just like Christian."

Jonny makes a face, laughing with her. "You mean

he sounds like me. I taught the man everything he knows about sailing, you know."

"My point is, that's how he feels, and I hate sailing. We had a big fight, when he realized I hate sailing and would never be willing to get on a sailboat with him and sail away and never come back, which is what he always dreamed of us doing."

She pauses for a while and resumes, explaining the story once more. "He stayed in Ft. Lauderdale for me. With me and *for* me. He gave up the sea for me. But I think deep down he always felt a little imprisoned. Trapped, sort of. So to him, he was like the selkie in his story, except instead of being the woman who lets him go back to the sea where he belongs, I stole his skin and trapped him on land with me. The story is his attempt to make sense of why he left me like he did. When Henry . . . ah, um—when—when . . ." She trails off, choking. Starts over, stronger. "When Henry passed away, grief sort of . . . took over. I checked out, basically, and he was left to deal with his own grief totally alone. Eventually, he had to go. He *had* to. Like a selkie, if he didn't go back to the sea, he would have wasted away."

Jonny nods. "Makes sense, when you explain it like that."

He meets my gaze then, and I think I understand Ava, and I feel, also, like that story can be applied to Jonny and me. He's as much a selkie as Christian is, he belongs out there, and I have my life here, and it would be the worst kind of cruelty to trap a man like Jonny on land with me, like Murtagh in the story. It makes sense, when seen through the lens of Christian's story.

Jonny's eyes, on mine, shine with an understanding, a mutual moment where each of us realize the truth we're both wrestling with.

Ava sighs. "If he's out there, he'll come back to me."

"Don't give up hope, though, okay? Our boy is a fighter, you know?" Jonny passes a hand through his hair. "Now that you're feeling a little better, I think I'd better, uhh . . ." He shrugs. "I should go. I gotta find Dominic." He stands, glancing at me, then away, and back to me.

Trying not to look too hard at me. Trying not to let me see what he's feeling.

I do see it though.

"I'll walk you out," I say.

Ava glances back and forth between Jonny and me, speculative. Suspecting. I hustle after Jonny and walk him to the hospital exit. We stand face to face, surrounded by a swirl of people: nurses, EMTs, and people visiting loved ones.

Neither of us seems to know what to say.

Jonny reaches up, touches my face with his palm. "I guess this is *adios*, huh?"

"I guess so."

He hesitates, his palm still on my cheek, and lets out a frustrated breath.

And then he kisses me.

It's not a goodbye kiss, it's . . . it's an everything kiss. Desire, regret, need, goodbye, an expression of a million things neither of us know how to encapsulate in our thoughts, much less say out loud.

I break the kiss first, because my throat feels oddly tight, and there's a lump that feels hot and hard, and it's so stupid to feel any of this, so I break the kiss, back away laughing, wiping at my lips. "You're such an asshole," I say.

He frowns. "How so?"

"By not being an asshole." I take another step back. "And for kissing me."

"Sorry for not being more of a dick, I guess?" He laughs. "But sorry, not sorry for the kiss."

I dart back to him, three tripping steps that leave me pressed against him, in his arms, my hands buried in his messy hair, kissing the ever-loving hell out of him, and then I back away. Another step, and another, staring at him, fingers on my lips, feeling the memory of the kiss lingering there, and then I turn and go back into the hospital. And yeah, the entire way back in, I feel Jonny's eyes on my ass, and I may or may not have perhaps not so subtly accentuated the sway of my hips just for him.

When I get back up to Ava's room, she spends the first few minutes I'm back eyeing me.

"What?" I ask.

She wiggles a finger at me. "You and Jonny. There

was something in the air between you two."

It hurts, and I'm still fighting the urge to cry, and I really don't want to talk about it, especially not with Jonny's best friend's wife, who is my sister. I shrug.

"He's gone. Doubt I'll see him again."

Ava peers at me, her little sister eyes seeing too much. "You're trying not to cry."

"Am not."

Ava shakes her head. "I'm not an idiot, Delta. I know when you're trying not to cry. You won't look at me, you're swallowing a lot, and you're blinking a lot, and you're using that clipped I-don't-want-to-talk-about-it tone of voice."

I sigh. "Okay fine, well . . . I don't want to talk about it."

She sits up a little higher. Eyes me even more suspiciously. "Delta . . .? Did you sleep with Jonny Nuñez?"

I shrug again. "Does it matter? He's gone."

Ava wraps an arm around me. "Oh God, honey. You slept with a sailor."

I can't help sniffling, and I hate myself for it, because this is classic Stage Five Clinger syndrome in full bore.

"You fell in love with him too, didn't you?" she asks.

I shake my head. "It's nothing like that."

"Then why are you crying?"

"Because I'm a dumbass."

"You've always been a dumbass, dumbass. I watched you go through a dozen breakups, and you never cried.

You didn't cry when everything happened with that rich asshole Tom or whatever his stupid name is, and you haven't cried since. But you're crying now." She huffs a laugh. "You fell in love with him, silly."

"Did not."

"Did too."

"Did not!" I snap.

She just laughs. "Did too." She points at me and ticks off her fingers as she lists things to prove her point: "Tears, don't want to talk about it, denying it left and right—all classic signs of love."

"I don't believe in love: number one," I say, ticking things off on my own fingers now, "and we barely know each other: number two, and we live totally and completely incompatible lives: number three."

"None of that has any bearing on whether or not you fall in love with someone. Love isn't logical, honey."

I glare at her. "You're not helping, Ava." I wave a hand. "Besides, he's gone, and he's not coming back. It doesn't matter if I did or not."

Ava just holds me until I'm able to get my stupid bullshit under control, and then she smiles brightly at me. "So. You mentioned a bonfire and singing? Think they'll have another one tonight?"

I smile back and nod. "Rob said they were going to."

She gestures at the hospital room. "Well? Help me blow this popsicle stand, huh? I need clothes, and I need real food, and I want to hear you sing."

I breathe out shakily. "Some of that is easier said than done, but we can figure something out."

"I don't care if I have to go hungry and wear this stupid hospital gown, as long as I get to hear you sing, Delta."

I hug her again. "I can manage that much, I think."

6

I t's well past midnight, maybe nearing on one in the morning. Dominic is beside me. We're sitting on the edge of the boardwalk, in the shadows. A dozen feet away, maybe less, is the bonfire. There are at least a hundred people sitting in groups, or couples, or individuals, all gathered around the fire. The audience is in a semicircle, focused on a single point, four people with their backs to the fire, facing the crowd.

Rob, Elaine, Corey . . . and Delta. I've been here since darkness fell, sitting in the shadows, listening. I found Dominic easily, but instead of staying on his ship, my feet somehow carried me here, and Dominic, being the man he is, followed me without question. I have been sitting in the darkness for hours, listening to Delta. Ava is with her, sitting off to one side, wearing obviously borrowed clothing, looking sad but momentarily distracted.

Delta has that effect, I'm discovering. She's . . . mesmerizing. Put that guitar in her hands, and she transforms completely. She opens her mouth to sing, and she's a whole different person. Rob, Elaine, and Corey all seem to realize this, seem to understand there's something special about Delta, about the way she sings. They all manage to shine as musicians, but none shine as brightly as Delta. She doesn't just shine, she . . . *mierda*, I don't know to put it. She glows from the inside out when she's singing.

They've done so many songs I don't know how they know them all, where the memory for all those chords and words comes from. Now the song they're doing ends and the last notes fade into silence. No one applauds, because they're all rapt, waiting for more.

Rob, mandolin in hand, nudges Delta's foot with his. "You have any original songs?"

"Yeah, but—" she starts.

"Do one for us," Rob suggests, cutting in over her protest.

At this, the gathered crowd howls and cheers, but Delta just shrugs.

"I haven't performed my own material in a long time," she says, stroking the strings of her borrowed guitar.

"So?" This is Corey, the dreadlocked drummer.

"You're a fuckin' rock star, D. You got this. Let's hear something you wrote."

Ava leans close to Delta, whispers something, and Delta argues back in a fierce whisper. This goes on, back and forth, until Delta finally hisses in frustration.

"Fine! I'll do the damn song if it means so much to you. Jesus, Ava, you're so damn persistent!"

Ava does a cutesy smile. "What else are little sisters for?"

There's one of those little clips on the end of the guitar, a capo I think it's called, and Delta fastens it to a precise spot on the fretboard, strums, adjusts the position of the capo minutely, and tries a few cursory chords. Then she adjusts a tuning peg, a different one, strums again, and nods. The tune is immediately familiar to me, and probably to everyone else in attendance; we've all heard it on the radio a million times.

"Um . . . a long time ago, I used to live in Nashville. I had this dream of being a famous songwriter and performer. Well, that didn't pan out, exactly. But I did sell a couple songs. You may have heard this one." She plays a few chords and laughs abruptly. "I guess anyone could sit here and claim to have written this song, but I swear I really did. I think you can probably google the copyright info if you don't believe me, but . . . shit, it's my song, and I'm gonna play it. I've never played this for an audience before so this is a first for me."

A pause.

"This is a song called 'Another Bar, Another Mic,'" she says.

Delta plays then, a familiar melody that's so simple, so compelling. She plays it a little slower than the artist on the radio, but to me it seems to work better this way. More . . . mournful, more haunting.

After a minute or two of playing the melody, Delta begins to sing. Before, singing other people's music, she shone, she glowed. Singing her own music? *Jesus Cristo*, she . . . she's on fucking fire.

"Truck stop diner outside Miami
Got my good jeans on, favorite cami
Guitar in the front seat beside me
and another gig behind me
Got a bad boy habit
an addiction I just can't beat
Burns hotter than whiskey neat
Wash my hands
but it don't wash the bad boy off me
So I slide on in, get another coffee
I know it's gonna hurt
but that don't stop me
They do me wrong
and I put 'em in a song

Every night it's the same old thing
Another bar, another mic

Another hey pretty thing
Lemme hear you sing
Another hey little mama,
Let's cut the drama
Another town and one more gig
Another beer and one more swig
Another hotel bar and a good lookin' liar
Another one-night stand and a drunk dial

I've got another gig tomorrow
Another night to sing my sorrow
because I'm just a six-string singer
and a first-light leaver
I'll sneak out while you're sleepin'
And creep out while you're dreamin'
I'll love you hard and leave you reachin'
I'll love you fast and leave you weepin'

Truck stop diner outside Miami
Got my good jeans on, favorite cami
Guitar in the front seat beside me
and another gig behind me
Got a bad boy habit
an addiction I just can't beat
burns hotter than whiskey neat
Wash my hands
but it don't wash the bad boy off me
So I slide on out, get another coffee

Take it to go and hit the highway
This is my life and I live it my way
I know it's gonna hurt
but that don't stop me
They do me wrong
and I put 'em in a song

Every night it's the same old thing
Another bar, another mic
Another hey pretty thing
lemme hear you sing
Another hey little mama,
Let's cut the drama
Another town and one more gig
Another beer and one more swig
Another hotel bar and a good lookin' liar
Another one-night stand and a drunk dial

I've got another gig tomorrow
Another night to sing my sorrow
because I'm just a six-string singer
And a first-light leaver
I'll sneak out while you're sleepin'
and creep out while you're dreamin'
I'll love you hard and leave you reachin'
I'll love you fast and leave you weepin'."

The applause is wild, with scattered whistles and

a lot of howling and cheering. I've heard that song on the radio so many times, and to think that Delta wrote that. It has her mark all over it, the brutal honesty, the unapologetic bluntness, a hint of self-deprecation and a sense of regret. It's all her. It's *so* her.

When the applause dies down, eventually, Delta seems stunned. Both at the warm welcome of the crowd, and the fact that she just performed that song. She's emotional, smiling with her palm flat on the strings, staring around her, just drinking in the moment. There's someone recording this via cellphone, I notice, and I'm glad this moment won't be forgotten.

My heart hurts, watching her. I don't want to leave, don't want to miss her, but I know this can't happen; it can't work.

Dominic nudges me. "Best get outta here, Jonny." His voice is pitched low, so only I hear him. "You're only dragging it out, brother."

I nod. "I know. I know." Blowing out a breath, I stand and ignore the way my soul is screaming, reaching out, reaching back to Delta. I walk with Dominic down the boardwalk, away from the fire. Away from Delta. Away from what my heart and my soul and my body all agree is the best thing I've ever had.

Within half an hour, *Glory*, as Dominic calls her, is bobbing through the gentle swell of the incoming tide, arcing eastward away from the coast and then northward toward Charleston. It's well after dawn before I find the bunk Dominic told me is mine, and though I'm glad to have the sea under me again and the soothing sound of water around me as I drift off, sleep is slow in coming.

I'm thinking of Delta.

I wonder if Jonny thinks I didn't notice him out there, in the shadows? He sat in the darkness outside the light of the fire for hours, listening to Rob and the rest of us play. There was a man with him, tall, built like a brick shithouse, with long dark hair and a thick beard. Dominic probably, the owner of the boat that rescued Jonny. They just sat there, listening. Jonny thought I didn't see him, but of course I did. I pretended like I didn't, just to make it easier on the both of us. But I felt him. I felt his attention. And I feel it now as he leaves, following my performance of my song.

I want to cry when he leaves, because I know it's the last time I'll see him. I don't cry, though. Instead, I do a song I wrote to myself when I was pregnant with

Alex and feeling lonely.

"I have another one, if you wanna hear it," I say. There's applause and a gesture from Rob, who seems to be our de facto leader. "No one's ever heard this song, except maybe my son, so . . . yeah. Here it is. It's called 'Until It's Gone.'"

I play the melody, and the words flood through me, like they always do once I start a tune.

"Don't cry, don't cry, don't cry
It won't take the hurt away
It won't wash the pain away
Keep your chin up and just hold on
Just keep breathing till it's gone

So what if he never loved you
Who cares if he just used you
His kisses abused you
His beautiful body unglued you
His charm subdued you
And then he walked away,
and screwed you.

Don't cry, don't cry, don't cry
It won't take the hurt away
It won't wash the pain away
Keep your chin up and just hold on
Just keep breathing till it's gone

So what if you're all alone
I know, I know
You're not made of stone
It's okay to be broken
Take a moment, so what if it's stolen
These midnight tears won't mend you
This heartbreak won't end you

Don't cry, don't cry, don't cry
It won't take the hurt away
It won't wash the pain away
Keep your chin up and just hold on
Just keep breathing till it's gone."

I breathe through the shakiness and the throbbing heat in my throat, as the last notes quaver in the silence. There's a long, tense moment of silence, people sitting in the sand staring at me. A few people are crying. Shit, I'm crying. I'm feeling the lonely ache I felt then, and it's deepened by the pang of Jonny finally, truly walking away. I knew he would, I knew he had to go; I knew he couldn't and wouldn't stay. I knew our lives couldn't fit together. But none of that has any bearing on the fact that . . . I don't want him to go.

There's an explosion of applause, and I realize the crowd has grown somehow. There's someone at the front of the crowd, close to Rob, Elaine, Corey, and me, and he's recording us with his cell phone. He has a mini boom-mic attached to his phone to better capture the sound. It feels good to be in front of a crowd again, to have a guitar in my hands, to use my voice, to sing my own songs.

I feel alive again, after feeling half-dead for so long—more than half-dead . . . mostly dead, barely alive, barely subsisting. Scraping by day to day, focusing on Alex and getting through each shift, each day.

Rob starts a Punch Brothers song, and I play along with the melody and let Rob sing. His rough and gravelly voice is nothing like Chris Thile's, but there's a genuine quality to Rob's voice that's distinctive and compelling, making everything he does deeply personal and meaningful.

Another song, and another one, and then the black of night is beginning to give way to a touch of gray, and people are yawning and falling sleep where they sit in the sand, and Rob announces we're done for the night. Elaine, once again, vanishes without a word, carrying her cello and bow as if she doesn't have a case for them, and Corey flits away to mingle with some people he seems to know, lighting up a joint and walking down the beach to smoke it with them.

Rob stays where he is, fitting his mandolin into a case and latching it. He glances at me as I linger, reluctant to give him the guitar. I'm playing still, picking out an idle melody I've had running through the back of my head.

"You know, Delta, you never mentioned your last

name," Rob says.

I frown at him, wondering why it matters. "Martin. Delta Martin."

He nods. "I wondered."

My frown deepens. "What do you mean?"

He shrugs. "Well, there ain't that many singer-song-writers out there named Delta, you know? So I figured you had to be Delta Martin."

"I'm not following."

He grins. "I'm a producer, honey. Cut my teeth in Nashville as a songwriter, switched to producing after selling a handful of songs, and I've been producing for going on twenty-five years. I knew I'd heard your voice before about halfway through 'Jolene,' but I couldn't place it. I get a lot of demos, and not a lot of them stick in my memory, but I remember your demo of 'Another Bar, Another Mic' as clear as day, and I swear you sound better now than you did then."

I laugh. "Thanks, I guess."

"I wanted that song and I wanted it bad, but I didn't have a performer with the chops to do it justice, so I had to let it go. Chapped my ass to let Bruce snap that up." He shakes his head. "Shit luck for you, too. I coulda made you a star. Bruce was a dipshit and a has-been, and had no eye for talent."

He was saying *was*, because Bruce—the producer who'd bought my song all those years ago—had passed away recently.

I shrug. "Bruce said he was gonna make me a star, but he didn't do shit for me. Sold a couple more songs, but it went nowhere. I just . . . I got no traction."

"Because Bruce was an idiot, God rest his soul. He didn't know what to do with you. He didn't know how to market the honesty in your song writing." He pauses, eyeing me with an odd look in his eye. "If you don't mind me asking, what is it you're doing now, if you're not in music anymore?"

I duck my head and dig in the sand with my toe, palm on the strings of Rob's guitar. "Um. I'm a waitress."

"That's a travesty, Delta," Rob says. "You are far too talented to be hauling a tray around."

I laugh again. "Rob, look at me. Look at what I'm wearing. I'm not just hauling trays, I'm hauling trays at a place that makes Hooters look classy. Washed up doesn't even come close, okay?"

He quirks an eyebrow at me. "You still writing songs?"

I sigh. "Sure. I can't seem to make myself quit, even though it ain't ever gonna turn into anything."

"How many do you have written?"

"Songs?" I splutter sarcastically. "I've been writing for more than twenty years, Rob . . . shit, I have hundreds."

"Hundreds? Like that one you just played?"

"I mean, yeah. They're mostly angry, angsty, lonely, and bitter, but yeah."

"You should come to Nashville," Rob says. "We can

make another go at it."

I stare at him. "Not funny, Rob."

He stares back. "Who's joking? I'm retired, which is why I'm in Florida, but I'm not totally out of the game."

I squash flat the hope trying to blossom inside me. "Rob, for real. What am I gonna do in Nashville? Start the whole process all over again, at almost forty, with a six-year-old boy in tow?" I glance at Ava, who's sitting beside me, listening and watching silently. "And, oh yeah, a sister with a missing husband and a home that's now leveled."

Rob shrugs. "Delta honey, I can't make you do shit. I also ain't gonna promise you shit. But, what I *will* say is that if you give me two weeks in Nashville, record a couple songs for an EP, let me shop it around a little bit, you'll get traction. It's a new scene now, babe. Satellite radio, YouTube, and iTunes has changed everything since you were there. Makes it both harder and easier to get your music out there." He gazes intently at me. "You gotta at least *try*, Delta."

I choke back tears. Shake my head. "That dream is long dead, Rob. It would hurt too much to try only to be rejected all over again. I'm fine with my life."

Rob spits in the sand, a violent gesture of dis-agreement. "Bullshit!" he thunders. "That there is rife, rank bullshit. You are *not* fine with your life. You ain't washed up, and your dream ain't dead. You hit a detour. You gained experience. And yeah, maybe it won't go anywhere. God knows I can't see the future and can't make any guarantees, but I made a career on my ability to know when someone's got it, and baby girl, you've got it. You had raw talent as a twenty-year-old girl and now, as a thirty-some-year-old woman, you have that same raw talent, but you have . . . shit, I don't know the words for it. Gravity. A sense of sadness and sorrow that makes everything you sing feel more raw and real and deep. There's something there in the way you perform now, that wasn't there when you were a girl."

Tears trickle down my face, and I can't stop them. "Goddammit, Rob! You can't do this to me. You can't make me want it all over again." I shove his beautiful classic Martin into his hands and shoot to my feet, stomping across the sand.

I feel someone following me, and I assume it's Ava, but I don't bother looking. I angle into the waves, wade in up to my calves, and I let myself cry.

Whoever was following me sidles into the water beside me; it's Rob, the guitar still in his hands. He settles the strap over my head, hanging the guitar on me. "Let yourself want it, Delta." His voice is quiet, rough from a lifetime of whiskey and cigars and singing. "Take the dream back and let it grow. Go after it. Like I said, give me two weeks. A month, even. I know a guy who owns an apartment complex, so I can get you a deal on a nice place for cheap, and I know the managers of all the bars in Nashville, so I can get you a job slinging drinks on

Music Row if you end up wanting to stay.

"Record an EP with me . . . studio time is on me, okay? Because I *believe* in you. Your talent is something the world deserves to hear. Your boy deserves to know his mama can be more than a waitress at some shitty place barely more than a titty bar. I know you're doin' it for him. My mama did the same. Worked three jobs to feed me and my brothers and put a roof over our heads, and one of those jobs was dancin' at a titty bar. She didn't have your talent, though. You got the talent, and I'm givin' you the opportunity, so just take it, okay?"

I have a guitar in my hands, and I can't help playing it. My fingers pick out a melody as tears run down my face, and I sing the lyrics softly, almost in a whisper, mainly for myself.

"Don't look at me, baby boy
I don't want you to know
I don't want you to see
Where I go
Or what I do
Just to buy that toy
I don't want you to know
Baby, I don't want you to know

I wait till you're asleep
And I kiss your cheek
Tug the blankets up higher

Tuck you in tighter
It's just another day, just another week
Another night digging deep
Another night wearing a whole lotta not much
Working that late night rush
Dealing with the late night crush
Bending over too low
Putting too much on show
Letting all the drunks see
Too much of me

Don't look at me, baby boy
I don't want you to know
I don't want you to see
So don't look at me
I hope you never know
I hope you never see
Where I go
What I do, baby boy
Just to buy that toy
Don't look at me
Don't look at me
Because I don't want you to know
Baby, baby, baby, don't look at me
I don't want you to know
I don't want you to see

I do it all for you

You're all I've got
And I wanna give you everything
I know it ain't a lot
But it's all I can do
And I do it all for you
I do it all for you."

It pours out of me, a song I wrote a few months ago, when I'd come home from work late, and Alex woke up crying, wanting me. I was still in my work outfit and I stank of booze and cigarettes and I'd been propositioned twice—and I'd nearly accepted one of them, simply because he'd offered enough that I'd have been able to make rent *and* buy Alex the new shoes he needed. I'd turned him down, because hooking and stripping were the two things I refused to do, no matter how desperate I got.

It's just me and Rob, standing in the surf. He wraps his arm around my waist, squeezing me in hug that's part friend, part gruff uncle.

"See? That there is country gold. It's not the peppy nonsense drinking song, and it's not a sappy breakup love song. It's got meaning and it's got depth, but it's catchy." He pats me on the shoulder. "Think about it, Delta. Think hard."

He walks away, out of the surf and back toward shore to wherever it is he's been sleeping.

I chase after him. "Rob, your guitar."

He pauses, smiling at me. "Keep it."

I sputter. "Rob, this guitar, it's . . . it's worth more than everything I own put together."

He laughs. "Honey, listen. That guitar is my baby. I bought Gloria new thirty-two years ago, and I've played a million gigs in a million bars with her. I wrote twelve number one country songs on her, and I've never gone a day without playing her." He puts his hand over mine on the guitar. "Trust me when I say that what she's worth money-wise ain't even a speck of dust compared to what she's worth to me in terms of memory."

I try to pull the strap over my head. "Exactly, which I can't—"

Rob won't let me remove the strap. "Shut up a second, Delta," he says, gently but firmly. "I ain't askin', okay? You're takin' that guitar, and you're gonna write me six brand new songs on her so we can put out your first EP. You're gonna be a goddamn star, and you're gonna do it playing my Gloria."

"I can't," I breathe. "I can't. It's too much."

"You can, and you will."

Ava is beside me, pressing against my side, resting her head on my shoulder. "Delta. Honey. Don't be stupid."

I choke out a sobbing laugh. "What? What do you mean?"

"I mean take the guitar. Let's you and me go get Alex from Mom and Dad, and take a trip to Nashville."

"What about—?" I have to start over. "What about

Ft. Lauderdale? What about Christian?"

She shrugs a shoulder. "I'm going to look for him. I have to. I just . . . I have to figure out how to go about it first. And in the meantime, I'll be with you and Alex."

I strum the strings, listening to Gloria's dulcet voice quavering across the surf. "One month," I say. "Then I'm going back to Chicago."

"You'll be on the radio giving interviews in a month, Delta," Rob says. "No more Chicago for you."

I sniff. "Good, because I don't have a job there, and the lease on my apartment is almost up." Another sniff and another laugh. "I'm homeless and jobless anyway, so I have nothing to lose."

Charleston, South Carolina
Three weeks later

I still got no ID, no passport, no money. Kinda wondering what the point is, anyway. I've spent the last few weeks with Dom and the boys on *The Glory of Gloucester*, trawling our way north to Charleston. It's good work, hard work, keeps my mind off everything. Off Delta. I mean, not much can keep my mind off her for long, but I'm fucking trying.

I work the nets from before dawn till after sundown. I always keep moving, keep working, keep busy. Don't sleep much, because if I sleep, I dream of her. If I'm idle, I daydream of her. I hear her voice, singing those songs. See her fingers, picking the strings. Feel her skin against mine. Her lips on mine. Her breast in my hand, her voice murmuring my name. I wake up hard as a rock most mornings, dreaming of her. I've woken up messy, having dreamed of her, of our time together on the beach, in the predawn light.

I've never been much for talking under the best of circumstances, unless I know you well and like you a lot. I got comfortable with Christian, and obviously Delta pulled something unique out of me, but with anyone else, I'm damn near mute. I'll shoot the shit with Dom up on the bridge late at night, on the long watches, but keep to myself otherwise. He's a lot like me, though, and we spend most of our time just sitting silent, sipping coffee, and watching the waves.

He knows what's eating me, I think, but he doesn't ask. I work, and he gives me a berth and feeds me. It's all I really need.

Only now that we're in Charleston for a bit, I'm going a little crazy. Or . . . a lot crazy. There's not much to do on board the boat when we're in port, which leaves me rattling around like a marble.

Eventually, Dominic takes me to a dive bar near the shipyards and buys me a whiskey. We sit at the end of the bar and drink for a while, and I wait, knowing he has something to say.

After the first glass, he taps the bar with a thick forefinger, shooting me a glance. "I been out there deep trawling for years. Only put into port for a few days here and there at the most. With Dane taking this apprentice-ship, I'm thinking I might hang around Charleston for a while. Make sure he's comfortable and likes the work before I head back out. Bully needs time to refit the engine and do some other repairs and upgrades anyway, and the rest of the crew can find temporary work easily enough. If necessary, I can always find new crew."

I sigh. "Spit it out, Dom."

He chuckles, tapping our glasses to indicate refills. After our glasses are topped off, he swirls the amber liquid in his glass, formulating his thoughts. "I don't wanna leave you in a bad spot, Jonny. You're a good man, and I consider you a friend."

"I'll figure somethin' out. Don't worry about me."

"That ain't how I operate." He takes a sip, hissing a breath at the burn. "You're damned miserable without her, Jonny. Might as well admit that much."

"Point being?"

"No point, just sayin'." He shrugs. "You're different since we left Florida. Way I see it, only a woman stuck in your craw can do that."

I laugh and shake my head. "She's not stuck in my craw, Dom. Forget about it, *amigo,* okay?"

Dom just gazes steadily at me. "Your berth is next to mine, and those walls are thin, pal. I hear you at night."

I frown at him. "Hear me what?"

"You talk in your sleep. Spanish mostly, but I've heard her name a time or two." He's not quite grinning when he says this.

I scowl. "Bullshit."

"I ain't above yankin' your chain, Jonny, but this is different. You say her name in your sleep."

"I do not." I breathe out a snarl and glance at him. *"Jesus Cristo,* do I really?"

"You do. Hand on my heart, swear to God." He puts his hand over his chest as he says this.

"Mierda." I lean back in the tall bar chair and toss a swallow of whiskey down. "I miss her, dammit."

"Right. So go back down and find her."

"She ain't gonna be there no more. Went back to Chicago, probably." I shake my head and shrug. "Nah, she's gone, Dom."

"Eh, you're just bein' a pussy."

I eye Dominic, my gaze hard. "'Scuse me?"

He crosses his burly arms over his chest, completely unintimidated. "I *said*, you're just bein' a pussy."

"How you figure?"

"You're scared. Yellow. Chicken . . . *Pussy.*" He grins at me. "Women'll do that to us, though. Turn the biggest, toughest, wildest man into a dumbass and a pussy and a landlubber homebody."

"I ain't no pussy."

He laughs. "Yeah, you are. If you weren't, you'd be lookin' for her. You wouldn't be wastin' your time on a rusty trawler with a bunch of ugly-ass bachelors and assholes if you weren't a pussy."

"*The Glory* ain't rusty. And you ain't ugly."

He laughs even harder. "Buddy, you're a pussy."

"I am *not*," I snarl.

"Then go look for her. Been three weeks and I think you've said a hundred words total. You work like a man possessed, and being a Latino, that means you're doing the work of four guys, at least. You, in the mood you're in? You could run the whole damn trawler by your damn self. Since we put into Charleston, you ain't left the boat until I dragged your grumpy ass here. You're avoiding the whole world, because somewhere in it is the woman you're hung up on, and you're too much of a pussy to put your heart out there and go after her."

"Fuck you." I say it again in Spanish, "*Andate a la cresta. Puta.*"

Dominic just chuckles. "Now, I don't speak Spanish, but I'm fairly certain that wasn't very nice." He taps our glasses for another refill. "I also don't think that was a denial."

I just sigh, and drink, and stare at the TV screen that is playing sports highlights. Somewhere, country music is playing on a local radio station.

After a while, Dominic tosses some bills on the bar, throws back the rest of his whiskey, and stands, patting me on the shoulder. "You know I'm right. Some things you just can't hide from, Jonny. You can run from the law, you can run from the IRS, you can run from crazy exes, shit, you can even run from your past. But you can't run from fallin' in love."

"You an expert, then?"

Dominic laughed. "Yes, I am. You know why I live on a deep-sea trawler and never see land, never see anyone but the ugly assholes on my boat? Because I was a pussy. I ran from falling in love, and I succeeded. By the time I realized I'd fucked up, it was too late."

I growl, because that was a pretty good answer. "Whatever. Stupid gringo."

He laughs yet again, even harder, and adds another pair of twenties to the pile on the bar. "Have another drink or three on me, Jonny, and think about it some."

Dominic leaves then, his gait the permanent rolling swagger of a burly man who's spent his whole life at sea. I mutter to myself in Spanish as I work on another glass of whiskey, cursing Dominic for being right, cursing Christian for disappearing and fucking everything up, cursing the hurricane, cursing myself, cursing Delta for being so damn tempting and tantalizing.

Another drink, and more cursing.

I switch to cheaper whiskey so I can drink longer. Stare at the TV and try to tune out the sappy country love songs playing in the background.

The more sappy country love songs and longing country breakup songs I have to tune out, the more angry I feel. This doesn't bode well. I get like this sometimes. I sit and drink way too much, and I let the deep, simmering sense of regret and unhappiness and loneliness that defines my life boil over, and it turns to anger, and I get into a stupid bar fight because I don't know how to deal with it.

My father left us when I was nine, which made me the man of the house at far too young of an age, with two sisters and a mother who was already working eighteen hours a day to make ends meet.

I went to work on the docks and helped take care of my sister and her kids and my mom. The first hurricane hit when I was eleven, and our house was flattened. We lost everything, moved, had to start over. Then another hurricane two years later flattened everything again, and we had to start over a second time. And then, a year later, yet another hurricane blasted across our little island, and that one was the worst one. It hit early in the morning, just before dawn. I was at the docks unloading fishing boats and moving fish. It hit the area where my mother and sisters and nieces and nephews lived, and I couldn't get to them. I tried, *mierda*, I tried. A stranger hauled me off the street and shoved me into a corner, pinned me down. I screamed through the whole damn storm, not because I was afraid, but because I knew what I'd find when I got home.

Our house was flattened. With my sisters and my mother and my sister's kids inside. They tried to hide, but there was nowhere to go, nowhere safe. I went mad, screaming, digging like someone possessed by a demon. I found them . . . too late.

Too fucking late.

That's when I hopped on-board the first fishing boat leaving the island that would take me away. That was the beginning of my life at sea, running from the loss of my family. Running from the pain. Running from my own cowardice. Never letting myself get attached to anyone, never staying in any one spot for long, or on any one boat for long. I lost the only family I had, and the thought of losing anyone else scares me to fucking death. It's defined my life in so many ways.

The anger at my life is boiling over. I've lost count of the number of whiskeys I've had. I gave the money Dominic left to the bartender and told him to keep giving me whiskey till the money was gone.

I don't want to be in love with anyone. It's stupid. I spent less than a week with Delta, and we only fucked a couple times.

Don't mean a damn thing. It was good sex, and I'm hung up on that. That's all it is. Love isn't real. I've fucked more women than I care to number, and none of them have ever stuck in my head like Delta. What is it about her? I don't fuckin' know. I don't know. I can't figure it out, and it's pissing me off.

The more I sit here, drinking and thinking, the more pissed off at the whole situation I'm getting.

The bartender refills my whiskey. "There's ten bucks left after this, bro."

I wave at him. "Keep it. I'm done."

He nods at me. "Thanks."

I nod sloppily and return my stare to the TV. The radio is still playing shitty annoying sappy country music, and I can't tune it out.

I'm thinking about trying to stumble back to the boat. I hit the head and drain my bladder, get a glass of water from the bartender and slam it, and two more after that. I make my way slowly to the door and the song ends, and the radio DJ comes on, probably in a pre-recorded segment.

"Coming up next is a brand new song, and let me tell you, it's a doozy. Her name is Delta Martin, and this song was released two days ago, and it's already rocketing up all the charts. And actually, she's not a newcomer to the country music scene. She's the writer behind several hits from the early part of the millennium, with songs like 'Another Bar, Another Mic,' 'You, Me, and the Night,' and 'Tall, Dark, and Handsome.' I don't really know where she's been the last ten, fifteen years, but if her comeback is gonna ride on songs like this, then watch out, folks, because she's on fire. This is Delta Martin, 'When Your Heart's Gone.'"

At the sound of Delta's name, I halt in place, hang my head, close my eyes, and grip the doorframe with one hand. I'm frozen, paralyzed.

The song starts, just Delta playing the guitar. Just her and the guitar, nothing else, a slow, mournful melody.

A slide steel joins in, adds a note of longing, and then a gentle, rolling drum beat adds urgency. And then I hear her voice, singing:

"You walked into my life, with your dark skin and
      brown eyes
I tried to resist you, tried not to kiss you
You speak soft and you move slow
You've got strong hands and few words
But I hear it anyway, everything you don't say
I tried to resist you, tried not to kiss you
But god, your lips, the way you moved your hips
The way you said my name
And said you felt the same
The way you took my hand
And kissed me in the sand

You said it won't work
I said it won't hurt
You said it's just for the moment, let's own it
What I didn't say was, here's my heart just break it
What I didn't say was, I'm feeling love, can't shake it
Baby, that was me lyin',
Because baby we shoulda kept tryin'
Now I'm sitting here without you
Wondering how do you go on
When your heart's gone
Because you walked away, said you can't stay

It was all too much,
God, it was more than lust
My heart's full of rust,
My soul's full of dust
It's such a rush,
It's more than a crush
More than your strong hands and slow sighs
More than your soft words and dark eyes
It's something I can't define
Something in your eyes, the way they shine
Makin' me want, makin' me wish
Makin' me moan, makin' me kiss
Makin' me groan, makin' me miss
Everything about you

I couldn't resist you, tried not to kiss you
But god, your lips, the way you moved your hips
The way you said my name
And said you felt the same
The way you took my hand
And kissed me in the sand

You said it won't work
I said it won't hurt
You said it's just for the moment, let's own it
What I didn't say was, here's my heart just break it
What I didn't say was, I'm feeling love, can't shake it
Baby, that was me lyin',

Because baby we shoulda kept tryin'
Shoulda kept tryin'
Now I'm sitting here without you
Wondering how do you go on
When your heart's gone
Because you walked away, said you can't stay."

I'm gutted. I sag against the doorframe of the bar, listening to the song. Hearing Delta's voice, the sorrow in it, the sweet, rich tone, the layers of emotion she can put into the words. Too fucking much, it's too fucking much. I shove out the door as the song ends, but I'm hearing it in my head over and over and over, hearing her words and knowing she meant them for me.

I barely remember getting back to the boat, and stumbling aboard. Instead of my bed, though, I end up on the bridge with Dominic, who doesn't say a damn word to me. He hands me a cup of coffee. He's kicked back in his captain's chair with a paperback in his hands. I just stare out the window at the night, the stars, and the lights of the shipyard, the water. Hearing Delta singing that song, over and over again in my head, on repeat.

Fuck.

I have to get out of here. I have to leave. I can't stay here.

I leave the coffee and head down to my berth to sleep off the whiskey.

This shit right here is why I sail. Out there, nothing

but the waves and the wind? There's nothing to hurt you, no one to make you feel things you never wanted to feel.

I pass out, grumbling to myself in Spanish.

New York City
One week later

I have a temporary ID finally, which lets me access my account in the Bahamas. It took some wrangling at the Columbian embassy, which meant hitching a ride on a freighter heading north to New York and walking halfway across the city to the embassy, but at least I'm an official person again.

I hear that damn song everywhere I go. It's gone viral. There's even a video. YouTube, I guess, but I haven't seen it yet. She's a bonafide viral sensation, apparently, and I'm pretty damn proud of her for that, even if my heart twists and aches every time I hear that fucking song.

I finally can't resist the temptation, so I buy some time at an internet cafe, pull up YouTube, type in her name and the song title.

Why am I doing this? What do I hope to accomplish? Add more confusion and pain? Make myself miss her and want her more? She's a star, now. They play that song on the radio every half hour, and it's even getting play on the pop stations since it has "crossover appeal," according to one DJ.

The computer finishes loading the page, and Delta pops up to fill the screen, the video playing automatically. It was filmed on a beach somewhere, not sure where. Dawn, the sea glassy and still. She's in a white sundress, knee-length, modest but sexy and beautiful. She has a guitar, looks like the one the guy from the beach let her use. She's gazing at the sea, playing the song and singing as the sun rises. The longing on her face is heart wrenching, the pain in her voice is just . . . it slices through me.

The song, the words . . .? *What I didn't say was, here's my heart just break it, what I didn't say was, I'm feeling love, can't shake it . . .*

I watch the video on repeat, because I can't seem to stop. Can't seem to figure out how to turn off the computer, how to get up, how to walk away, how to stop staring at the screen, at Delta, how to stop listening to her telling me she was feeling love, and I walked away.

I fucking walked away.

I had to, though, right? That was what we agreed to. We both knew there was no way anything could work. She said it, I said it, and there was no question.

My life is on the ocean. It's all I know. It's all I've ever known. What am I supposed to do? Learn a whole new life, a whole new trade? I'm a sailor; I sail.

Fuck this.

I tear off the headphones and storm out of the cafe,

leaving the song playing on the computer.

I'm feeling love, can't shake it.

No. It's not true. It's not. It's just not. That's only a clever line in a song.

I start out running but end up walking. I don't know where I end up, except it's at the water. The bay, late at night, moonlight and city lights glinting off the rippling water. There's a houseboat tied up nearby with the lights on. A couple sits on the front deck, her head on his chest, and his arm around her. There's a radio playing inside the cabin, and yeah, it's playing Delta's fucking song.

I groan in frustration and slump against the railing of the dock. I can't get away from the damn song.

It's like Fate is trying to make a point or something, putting Delta's song in my face everywhere I go. I don't believe in that shit, though.

I should just . . . go. Get on a trans-Atlantic freighter or something. Lose myself out there, where I belong.

Only, the farther I go, the more it feels like I belong somewhere else. I don't know where.

That's a lie.

I know where part of me wants to be, and that's wherever Delta is.

I don't know how to do that, though. I ran away after that last hurricane, when I was a kid. I ran because I couldn't save them, because I never could have, there was nothing I could do. I've run away my whole life, because it was what I knew. It's what I know. Ship to ship, shore to shore. Never still, never staying.

Hell, that could be a country song, couldn't it? Ship to ship, shore to shore, never still, never staying.

Maybe it's time to stop running and start staying.

Nashville, Tennessee

"**M**ama? When are we going back to Chicago?" Alex is in a booth across from me, eating French fries.

We're between recording sessions, finishing up the EP. Rob is working like a crazy person, acting as part manager and part producer, working like crazy to capitalize on the frenzy surrounding "When Your Heart's Gone," pushing the video, pushing the radio play, setting up a tour.

Setting up a tour? What? Me? Hell no.

But yes, he really is. Says Miranda needs an opening act for a handful of dates, and so does Carrie, and a few others, and if he can stitch the dates together just right and nail it all down, we'll have a killer debut tour on our hands.

I sip at my iced tea, chewing on the straw. "Not sure, baby."

He frowns at me, dipping his fry into ranch dressing. "I miss my friends. I wanna go home."

"We were going to move anyway, I told you that already."

"I know, but . . ." he trails off, shrugging. "I don't understand what's happening."

"Me either, honey-buns." I steal one of his fries and pop it into my mouth. "What would you think if we never went back to Chicago?"

He stares at me. "And stay here? In Nashville?"

I shrug. "Maybe. Or we might live on a big bus and travel all over the country." I pause, watching his reaction. "Mama could be a famous music star, baby. What do you think of that?"

He wrinkles his nose. "Really? So you wouldn't be a waitress no more?"

I sigh. "That's the idea."

"And you'd be famous? Like for really real? Famous like Tony Stark?"

"Could be"—I laugh—"although, Tony Stark is a fictional character, and last I checked, I'm real."

His blue eyes—my eyes, Ava's eyes, Mom's eyes— examine me carefully, thoughtfully. His blond hair is a little too long, shaggy on top and curling at the neck, but it looks cute on him, and he likes it, so I've been leaving it. "Would you not be sad anymore, if you get famous?"

I tilt my head, frown at him. "What makes you think I'm sad, baby?"

"*Mom.*" He rolls his eyes at me. "You're *always* sad. You play your guitar and sing sad songs when I'm sleeping. I like to wake up and listen."

"Baby, it's just—"

He interrupts me. "Will you get a famous boyfriend?"

"What?"

"You're all alone," he says. "My friend at school, back in Chicago I mean, Melissa, you know her. She says her mom has a new boyfriend every month, but they never stay around long, and my other friend Will, he says *his* mom never has a boyfriend, but she comes late from work sometimes acting weird and crying and stuff. Did you ever have any boyfriends? I thought if you got a famous boyfriend, you wouldn't be alone."

"I'm not alone, baby, I have you." I swallow back tears and emotion so he doesn't see it. "I don't need a boyfriend."

He finishes his fries and picks up a crayon, scribbles aimlessly on the paper under the plate. "Your song on the radio, it sounds like you're singing it to a boyfriend."

"Alex, listen—"

"If we live on a bus, does that mean I won't have to go to school anymore?"

"I can't keep up with you, buddy." I sigh. "If we live

on a bus, you'll have a tutor."

"Dang it. I thought I wouldn't have to learn no more."

"You have to learn, Alex, that's how you become smart."

"Did you go to college, Mama?"

"No, but that's not—"

"And you're pretty smart, aren't you? So why do I have to have a tutor? I can just watch PBS."

I laugh. "I *did* finish high school, kiddo, so I learned *some* stuff, but I do wish I'd gone to college. And no, you can't just watch PBS. I'm not sure we'd get PBS on the bus anyway. And all this is beside the point, since I'm not sure that's happening anyway. I just . . . I don't think we're going back to Chicago. That's my point."

"So could I stay with Gramma and Grampa in St. Pete's sometimes? That was fun! I got to have cake for breakfast once, and Grampa made pancakes like *every day*, and they let me have Coke whenever I wanted." He frowns, stopping abruptly and staring at me in something like panic. "Um. I mean—I had broccoli every day, and *never* had any sweets. So . . . I wouldn't mind staying with them sometimes."

I laugh. "Buddy, even if I didn't already know that your grandparents spoiled you rotten while you were staying with them, you still couldn't live with them."

"Why not?"

"Because you're my son, and I'd be sad without you."

"Oh. So I'm kinda like your boyfriend."

"Noooo, you're kinda like my *son*."

"What about Auntie Ava?" he asks, still tracing the crayon in idle circles. "If we go on a bus, and you're a famous music star, what will Auntie Ava do? Is she gonna be famous too?"

"She's . . ." I haven't really addressed the situation with Christian being missing with Alex just yet. I don't really know how to start that conversation with a six-year-old. "I don't know. She's . . . she has her own life, buddy. She's just spending time with us for a while."

"Where's Uncle Chris?"

Here it is.

I sigh. "Um. Well, actually, buddy . . ." Alex hears something in my voice and looks up at me, alert to what comes next. "Uncle Chris is . . . he's kind of . . . he's missing."

Alex is quiet a moment or two. "He's missing? Where'd he go?"

God, there's so much to explain. "Um. Well, we don't know. That's why he's missing."

"I don't understand."

"He was on a sailboat, and there was a storm, and now he's missing."

"Is . . . is he . . . is Uncle Chris dead?"

I sigh, taking his hands. "I hope not. Right now, he's just missing."

"Are people looking for him?"

So many questions I don't know how to answer.

"I . . . yeah, there are people looking for him."

Alex thinks about it for a bit and nods seriously. "Uncle Chris is pretty smart. They won't find him; he'll find them."

I smile at his confidence in his uncle. "I think you're right, buddy." I pay the bill and extend my hand to him. "Come on, kiddo. Mr. Rob is probably waiting for us back at the studio."

We walk back to the studio, and Alex glances up at me. "Mama?"

"Hmmm?"

"Can I be on your album? I can sing real good!"

And he shows me how good he can sing, going through the theme songs of half a dozen of his favorite shows, then goes into renditions of his favorite radio songs, and damn, the boy can actually sing like an angel. When we get to the studio, Alex repeats his request to Rob, and Rob indulges him, letting him sit on the stool in the recording booth and sing into the mic for a while, and even hits the playback button so Alex can hear himself singing.

"I don't sound like that!" Alex says, upset. "That's not how I sound!"

I laugh. "Our voices sound different in our heads than they do to other people," I tell him. "It's always weird to hear a recording of yourself."

He frowns and crosses his arms. "I don't like it. You

can be the music star, Mama. I'm gonna be an astronaut."

Rob and I both laugh as Alex stomps seriously out of the recording booth and takes his place on the chair in the production area with the iPad Rob gave him, watching *Paw Patrol* as Rob and I get back to recording the last song on the EP. It's going to be just me, my guitar, and a new song, one I just finished writing the other day. No band, no production, just a raw cut.

We do half a dozen different cuts before Rob calls a stop and comes in to talk to me in the booth. "I don't think this is the right song. It's a little *too* raw, too much emotion. That's a song you should only do live, to really show people what you've got. It just . . . it don't translate right, without the visual of you singing it. We could do a video for it, but honestly I think the best video for that song would be a concert cut of you singing it on stage, really pouring your heart out. Either way, it's not the song to close out the EP."

"So . . . what do we do?" I ask.

Rob shrugs. "I have a couple ideas. You can write somethin' else totally new, or you can demo me some of your older stuff, and we can pick one."

I nod, thinking. "I have a couple songs in mind. If you give me a little time, I can work up some demos for you."

Rob shakes his head. "Nah. Just play 'em. We won't isolate the vocals and guitar for this last one. Just play me a few songs, and I'll record 'em, and we'll pick the best cut. Play from your heart, honey, that's when you're best."

He mics my guitar and I spend a few minutes just fooling around, mentally going through some of the songs I've written over the years.

"I think I've got one," I say, and fiddle with the strings, trying to remember how the chords went. "Do we have any tour dates?" I ask to buy time; I still don't quite believe it's real, that an actual tour opening for actual country artists could really happen.

Rob just grins. "We do. I've nailed down six dates so far. The first one is in three days, actually. Opening for Miranda in New York City."

I squeal, hunching over my guitar and kicking my feet excitedly. "Seriously? Six dates?"

He grins even wider, leaning on the glass. "I have several more coming, just have to figure out the particulars. This tour is going to put you in the stratosphere, babe. You'll be a headliner before you know it."

I shake my head. "I can't even think about that, Rob. It's too much. None of this feels real."

"It is real, though. Really real."

"I know, I know." I sigh. "I just . . . it's surreal."

Rob smiles. "I know. I've seen it a hundred times. Advice from an old dog, honey? Don't ever get used to it. Always be amazed." He leans back, keeping his finger on the button. "Keep that fresh-eyed excitement. Stay passionate. That's what'll translate into stardom. You have all the talent in the world, Delta, you just needed the right break."

I'm choked up, trying to breathe through it and failing. "Why, Rob? Why are you doing all this for me?" My voice breaks on the last word.

He shakes his head, and his smile turns from encouraging and wise to compassionate. "Because I believe in music, honey. I believe that if someone has the kind of raw talent you have, they owe it to the world to use that talent, to share the music with the rest of us. The world deserves to hear the music you have inside you, Delta. I feel like it's my duty to get that music out there."

"What if no one likes me? What if I fail? What if I get up on stage in front of a real crowd for the first time, and I bomb? What if . . . what if I'm nothin' but a one-hit wonder?" Doubts pour out of me faster than I can verbalize them. "What if I just suck? What if I put out this EP and it doesn't move any copies? What if Alex hates it on the road and I have to stop touring? He has to come first, Rob. I can't and I won't sacrifice his future for my stupid dreams."

Rob lets go of the button, leaves the production booth and comes in to stand in front of me. He takes my face in his hands with the gruff gentility of a loving grandfather. "That there is fear talkin', honey-pie. Shut that shit down. People love your first single. They love your voice, they love your lyrics, they love the video . . . they love *you*. That song is rocketing up the charts, okay? The Highway picked it up for their On the Horizon program, and people went apeshit for it. Before you know, it'll be charting on the top thirty. You've *got* it, Delta.

"If you fuck up, you just smile and apologize and play your goddam guts out anyway." He lets go and backs up a step, gesturing at Alex, visible through the window, absorbed in his show, oblivious to this conversation. "And if he hates touring, you figure something out. I don't have all the answers, babe; I'm just your producer. All I know is I'm damn good at spotting talent and making it pop out there in the big ol' world, and that's what I'm gonna do with you. So stop overthinkin' everything." He squeezes my shoulder. "Now. Play me a song. Nothin' too heart wrenching, but not too peppy either. Somethin' catchy and commercial."

I blow out a shaky breath. "Okay. Okay. You're right." I strum an open chord, pick a few strings. "Catchy and commercial."

I find the right song, find the right chords, try to remember the melody and the lyrics. "This one is called 'Just Need Tonight,'" I say.

> "You got me like whiskey
> So baby just kiss me
> Tip me back and drink me down

Pick me up, take off my gown
I ain't no Cinderella, no fancy glass shoes
You ain't no Hollywood fella, on a list of who's who
So just pay the tab
Call us a cab
I've had a few drinks, can you taste 'em
Don't have many hours, so don't waste 'em
You got me like whiskey
All you gotta do is kiss me
Tip me back and pour me down
Pick me up and take off my gown

Don't need a pick up line
So don't ask me the time
I like whiskey, don't drink wine
Don't need salt, don't need lime
This ain't a date,
So baby don't wait
Don't mind the hangover,
Won't ask to stay over
Don't need a promise, don't need a call
All I want is this, baby that's all
Sweaty skin and whiskey lips
Beat of your heart and hands on my hips
Bodies in motion, shadows like oceans
Touch like devotion, kiss like a potion
You got me riled, so baby be wild
No number to dial, just keep me a while

Don't need tomorrow, just need tonight
I ain't no virgin, don't wear white
Take me out and show me around
Pick me up, show me the town
Butter me up, I might go down
Don't need my number, ain't a booty call
This ain't love, and I won't fall
All I want is you and me naked
Take me to bed, I won't fake it
Baby just get me screaming
And then leave me dreaming
Won't hear me weeping
This ain't love, I don't want keeping
Here comes the sun
Baby, it sure was fun

Don't need a pick up line
So don't ask me the time
I like whiskey, don't drink wine
Don't need salt, don't need lime
This ain't a date,
So baby don't wait
Don't mind the hangover,
Won't ask to stay over
Don't need a promise, don't need a call
All I want is this, baby that's all
Sweaty skin and whiskey lips
Beat of your heart and hands on my hips

Bodies in motion, shadows like oceans
Touch like devotion, kiss like a potion
You got me riled, so baby be wild
No number to dial, just keep me a while."

I end the song and glance at Rob to gauge his reaction. He nods, leans back in his chair and fiddles with dials and buttons for a while, lost in thought. After a minute or so, he leaves his side of the glass and comes over to mine, bringing a chair with him. He sits across from me with the chair reversed so he's straddling it with his arms resting on the chair back.

"Delta, can I be honest with you?"

I nod. "I hope you always will be, Rob."

"A lot of your songs have a running theme to them, I've noticed." He sighs, tapping the chair with a finger, hesitating. "You, just looking for a good time for the night."

I shrug, half-nod. "More or less. A lot of the songs guys write are about drinking and picking up girls, and I decided I wanted to write from the opposite perspective—that we girls like to have fun, too."

He nods. "I get that, I do. I just . . . I'm not sure that's the image you necessarily want to go for."

"What image, Rob? The slutty one?" I talk over his protests. "It's who I am, and I'm not going to apologize for it. I lived my life hard and fast until I had Alex, and a lot of my material came out of that. Trying to accept who I was, trying to figure it out, come to terms with it. My image won't ever be squeaky clean and shiny, because there ain't a single thing about me that's squeaky clean and shiny."

Rob holds up his hands to slow my tirade. "And sweetheart, I get all that. I ain't asking you to change, or to apologize, or to be anything you're not."

"Then what are you asking, Rob?"

"I'm asking you to dig deeper. As a songwriter, as a musician, dig deeper. Find me the song that tells a story, tells me as the listener something I can identify with, something that makes me feel."

"You said catchy and commercial, and that song felt catchy to me."

He nods. "It is. It's a damn good song, and I plan on fine-tuning it for later. But to end this EP, you need something that captures a part of who you are."

I blow out a breath and nod.

I've had something rumbling around my head for a while, and I play the chords as they come to me. I grab the notebook and pen on the floor by my feet and work out the lyrics. Rob is patient, willing to chat with Alex and wait me out. It doesn't take me long to fall into the spell of song writing, strumming a few chords, testing transitions, playing with tempo and phrasing and melody until I feel the song fall into the groove.

After ten or fifteen minutes, I feel confident that I have it down, and I play the melody through a few times, thinking through the lyrics. I feel it, now. Whenever I write a song, I have to work through it and figure it out, and then suddenly I feel something just . . . *click*. The moment when the song becomes a complete entity, no longer only an idea in my head but a real physical thing, there's this mental, emotional, physical *click*, when I know it's complete. It's not always fast, sometimes I have to work on a song for hours or days or even weeks before the click comes, and sometimes, like with this one . . . it's a matter of minutes, of letting the song pour out of me into what it's meant to be.

"I think I'm gonna call this one 'Faking This,'" I say, as I play a short music intro, and then start in on the lyrics. As I start singing, I let myself really feel it, let the emotions take over, let myself really miss Jonny, and I put all that into the way I sing, giving myself over to it completely.

"If I take this moment, will there be any more?
If I let you go, can I watch you walk out the door?
If I take this moment and own it,
It'll be the end of us, won't it?
There's a million reasons why written in the sky
They gleam like the moon
They tell of you leavin' me soon
A million reasons you can't stay
A million reasons you're walking away

If I just lie here in the dark maybe I'll dream of you
If I pretend my hand is your hand, maybe I'll scream
for you
If I close my eyes and wish, maybe I'll remember
your kiss
But I'm not all right, baby I'm just faking this

This won't be the end of me
So baby don't pretend for me
But did you have to look back?
The kisses, the whispers, was it an act?
The way you held me from night till the morning,
The way you took my heart without warning
Were they just lines, was it a game?
I said it's all too much, and you felt the same,
Your touch is more than a memory,
Your kiss, what it meant for me
Your words, what they did to me
Getting lost in the stars, it felt like a dream
You left and you're gone, was it what it seemed?
Did you love me, or were we just sex
Do you love me, or am I an ex?

If I just lie here in the dark maybe I'll dream of you
If I pretend my hand is your hand, maybe I'll scream
for you
If I close my eyes and wish, maybe I can remember
your kiss

But I'm not all right, baby I'm just faking this
I'm just faking this, faking this, faking this . . ."

The last note quavers in the booth, and I feel it echoing inside me. I look up, and Rob is grinning ear to ear, pointing at me through the glass and then slow clapping.

He leans forward and hits the button. "That! Honey, that is *it!*" he hollers. "That's the one, babe."

"Okay, so should we go through it again?" I ask. "I feel like I could improve it in a few places."

Rob shakes his head. "Nope, that's it, just like it is. I'm not doing a damn thing to it. You and your guitar, your raw vocals and the feeling you put into it, that's all you need."

"Rob, you're crazy. You can't put that on the EP like that. It's the first time I even played it through. I literally just wrote it!"

He laughs. "And that's why it's perfect. I've been saying we need this to be raw and real. You don't need to be produced, babe, you just need to be recorded."

"Can't we go over it once more?"

He shook his head. "Nope. You'll lose the edge of the passion if you do it again. It's gotta hit with that ragged edge you gave it. It wasn't perfect, and that's why it *is* perfect. Your voice shook in a couple places, and I swear to God I *felt* how deeply you feel about that guy, whoever he was."

I sigh and try to put aside the feelings I unearthed.

"You're the expert."

Rob's eyes pierce a little too deeply. "I've been tryin' to keep you locked in on the music the last few weeks, 'cause I thought maybe that was what you needed. But, babe, it's been damn near a month since we left Florida, and you're still digging some pretty ragged hurt out of that situation you left down there."

"It doesn't matter."

With a glance at Alex, who is now playing a game of some sort, his tongue sticking out of the corner of this mouth, Rob once again joins me in the recording booth, straddling the chair. "Sure it does."

I shake my head. "No, it really doesn't. He's gone and I'm here. It was never going to be anything, and we both knew it."

"Don't make it hurt any less."

"No, that's for sure." I try to smile at him and only partially succeed. "It is what it is."

Rob growls. "That's a load of bullshit."

I frown at him. "What do you mean?"

"Folks say 'it is what it is' when they feel like there ain't shit they can do about something, but that don't mean you can shove the way you feel under the rug like it doesn't matter." He taps my guitar. "You can put your hurt into a song and sing your way to a number one hit, but that doesn't count as dealing with it, Delta."

"I don't *want* to deal with it. Dealing with it means thinking about it, and I'm doing a pretty damn good job of living in denial."

Rob shakes his head. "That's no good, Delta. It won't work."

"Yeah, well, it has so far." I pluck a string and adjust the tuning a touch. "It's worked my whole life."

"Just because it's what you've been doing don't mean it's working, honey." He tugs on his beard. "Listen, I know what I'm talking about, okay? I'm successful, and I've never been told I'm ugly, but I'm single, and why you think that is? Because I've always done the same thing you're doing. Ignore the hurt and hope it goes away. Shove it all under the rug and don't talk about it, don't deal with it, and it stops hurting so much, eventually. Pretend I'm fine, keep on going, act like all the shit I've been shoving deeper and deeper ain't eating a hole inside me. That shit ferments on you, Delta. Turns to acid, and burns a hole inside you."

"Rob, I can't just—"

"I ain't sayin' you gotta unload it all on me. I'm just a retired producer, what do I know? But I also hope we're friends." I start to protest again, and he holds up his hand to stop me. "I won't bore you with the whole story, but here's the short version. I was married for near on twenty years. Met her back in Texas, when I was a hungry young buck working the honkey tonks down that way, trying to bust out of the local scene. She was a stone cold fox, and I fell in love faster than fire burns paper. We had things good for a spell. I pushed out of Texas and got the attention of some folks here in Nashville, and we got married, moved here. Kept writing and eventually got into producing and realized that was where my real talent was, more than writing or performing.

"For me and Lisa, though, it wasn't so golden. I got caught up in the excitement, made some mistakes, did some stupid shit that hurt her. And she retaliated in kind. Turned into this escalating thing we never acknowledged or talked about, just kept piling hurt on hurt until we forgot what our love looked like. We tried to fix it, tried therapy and all that shit, but it had soured until there wasn't anything left but old hurt. And the thing about old hurt you ain't dealt with, Delta? Just because it's old doesn't mean it's lost its potency. More often that not, just like whiskey, old hurt stings all the harder because it's old and all knotted up inside you."

I shake my head. "Rob, it's not the same. I met a guy, we had a fling, and it ended. That's it. Not worth dwelling on."

"Aw, now you're just talkin' out your ass and whistlin' Dixie, Delta." He stares hard at me, and I know he sees through me. "That lie don't sell, babe."

"Rob, goddammit." I rub the strings and set the guitar into the stand and put my face in my hands, sighing and scrubbing.

"It ain't just the boy, is it?" He jerks thumb at Alex. "And by boy, I don't mean that one. I mean the one who was watching you from outside the fire like he was fixin' to leave behind half his heart."

"It's . . . it's everything!"

"Well now, when you say it's everything, that can cover a whole lot of everything. Maybe try to narrow it down a mite?" He holds up a finger. "Hold on a second. I think we need some liquid honesty for this." He vanishes, comes back with a bottle of whiskey. "Looks like your little soldier there is getting sleepy, so why don't we take this conversation back to your place?"

So we end up in Rob's fancy little car, Alex in the tiny back seat, yawning and trying to act like he isn't. Rob did indeed find me a really nice apartment in Nashville, ground floor with a patio and good schools if we end up staying.

I had a little bit of money saved up, and I used it to pay a couple months of rent up front so I can focus on recording. If this gamble doesn't pay off, I'll be screwed, but I'll hate myself if I don't try, so I'm putting it all on the line and hoping.

Rob wanted to help with rent, but I drew the line there, because that was starting to feel a bit too much like charity, and even though I get the feeling Rob is a genuine person with genuine motives, I'm far too jaded to let myself be in any kind of financial debt to him. I'm not sugar-baby material, but a lonely older guy with money and a younger woman in a desperate situation? Yeah, I wasn't about to let him start paying my way in life. A guitar, sure. Some studio time, sure. He's part owner of the studio, so he's not losing money on this, as we're working around the schedules of other artists, wedging in time when the booth is free.

Thus, we end up at my apartment, Alex in bed, snoring before I get the blankets up to his chin. Rob has whiskey poured out in juice glasses and is sitting on my patio with one glass on the ground under his chair, feet kicked out, picking a slow, sweet melody on Gloria.

He sees me coming out and hands the guitar over. "Here. I was just playing her for old time's sake."

"She's your guitar, Rob."

He shakes his head. "Nah, I gave her to you. But I wouldn't mind if you let me play her now and again."

I take a drink and watch Rob play, envious of and amazed by his effortless mastery, the way he can make a simple melody so compelling. After a few minutes, he quiets the strings with his palm and lifts his glass to his mouth, takes a long sip, and eyes me.

"So. Everything, huh?"

I sigh. "Why do you wanna hear this, Rob?"

"Because we're friends. Because I want you to find your way to something better out of your life, emotionally speaking, and you can't get there by bottling it all up." He takes another drink. "And because you need a friend. Your sister has her own shit to deal with, and I get you aren't willing to burden her with yours."

"What do you get out of this, Rob?"

He laughs. "I spent my whole life thinkin' about me

and only me. I took what I wanted from Lisa, from my friends, from my clients, from everyone. I never invested in anyone or anything unless I could get something out of it. For my whole life, I was the one asking 'what's in it for me?' It got so bad Lisa left me, and then I had a health scare and ended up retiring earlier than I was planning, and then damn near died in that freak storm down in Florida.

"All that has me wonderin' if maybe I oughta start thinking about other questions, maybe start asking what I can give, rather than what I can get." Another laugh, a more cynical one. "Plus, if you succeed, I make money. And if you're happy, you're gonna make better music."

I frown. "What was it you said? You're talking out of your ass and whistling Dixie."

He chuckles and sips whiskey. "Nah, not exactly. Truth is, I like you. You remind me of me, just a whole hell of a lot prettier." His gaze as it flicks to me is sharp and insightful. "I hope I don't have to say this, Delta, but . . . I'm your friend. I'm your producer and sort of your manager. Ain't nothin' else."

I let out a breath, because I don't sense any duplicity in him. "I've been lonely my whole life."

"That's a long time to be lonely."

"Yeah. I had a dream, and I went after it. Busted my ass going for it, did everything right, everything I could. Kept myself free of entanglements, you know? I was laser-focused on making it, and there wasn't place in my life for anything else. But I just . . . I never made it. I *al-most* did . . . but it fizzled out.

"And then I was trying to survive and got knocked up by a random asshole and had Alex, and then it wasn't just survival, it was trying to give him everything I could. He's all I've got, that boy in there, and I'm all he's got. But . . . he's just a baby."

I sniff and cover it with a sip of whiskey, hissing at the burn. "My folks, Ava, Chris . . . what were they gonna do when I had Alex? Bail me out? Watch him while I try to revive my dead music career? Nah. They were there, they love me, I know that. My folks . . . they're flaky. They're focused on themselves. They weren't bad parents, but Ava and I both left home young because they . . . they kept us alive and we knew they cared about us, but they were . . . flaky. I don't know how else to put it. Don't get me wrong, I know I was lucky. I grew up with two parents in a middle-class neighbourhood—I had it easy. But I couldn't depend on them, emotionally. I couldn't rely on them, so I didn't."

And Ava and Christian were . . . I don't know. Chris's success was so meteoric I felt like I couldn't be a burden to them, and I wasn't about to take handouts from them, so I just . . . I stayed in Chicago and kept my head down and did what I had to do to take care of Alex."

"But that's all you ever did," Rob finishes for me.

"Right. All through my shot at music and ever since, I've been alone. I've never had a serious relationship, never. I dated this one guy for two months, when Alex was a baby. He knew I had a kid, and it seemed like he was cool with it. But then when it started to get more serious and we talked about him meeting Alex and spending time at my place rather than me going to his . . . he was like, nah, I'm good. He just bailed, dumped me before work one day. And I didn't blame him, honestly. I mean, yeah, it was a dick move, but I got it. It wasn't ever gonna go anywhere.

"That's all I've ever had. Quick and easy and cheap and shallow. Nobody has ever . . ."

I have to stop, because this more real than I've ever gotten with anyone.

I take a deep breath and start over. "No one has ever made me feel special. No one has ever made me"—I shrug—"just *feel*. Like, deep down. My songs are all about heartbreak and getting drunk and hooking up, because that's all I've ever known. I gave them what they wanted, but deep down . . . I've just . . . all I want is . . ." I can't quite finish the thought.

"Someone to give a shit," Rob fills in.

"Yeah," I laugh, through a sniffle, "someone to give a shit. And Jonny, I didn't know him long, but it felt like he gave a shit. He made me feel. More than just, you know, the sex stuff, wanting him and being attracted to him and all that . . . Jonny made me feel real emotions."

"Such as?"

"Fear. Need. Curiosity. Desperation. Helplessness." I

swallow hard. "He made me feel like . . . like I wasn't so alone."

"Now you're here, and he's . . .?"

I shrug. "I don't know."

I thought I was strong enough to handle the end of whatever Jonny and I were: more than a hook-up, less than a relationship—some fucked up amalgamation that wasn't quite one and wasn't quite the other. I'd known it was going to hurt, but I couldn't help taking what I could get from Jonny, because despite being all too brief and not quite enough and also far too much for the short time we had, it was better than anything I've ever known. Physically, it was incredible. Emotionally, it was . . . a tease.

Nowhere near enough.

I've been avoiding this realization for the last month, but now I can't ignore it anymore:

I miss Jonny.

Ironically, I'm exploding onto the music scene, getting the break I never thought I'd get. Success is in my grasp. I'm about to go on tour with some of the most famous country music stars in the world, and people are learning my name and the sound of my voice and the flow of my lyrics. I'm *making* it.

It's tempting to say it doesn't mean anything without Jonny, but that wouldn't quite be true, and I'm not really into unnecessary melodrama. I wanted this long before I met Jonny, and if I never see him again, this sudden and unexpected success will still be just as sweet.

But long term? Without Jonny . . . when the lights go out, when the recording studio is empty, when I'm alone in my bed, I'll still miss him. I'll still always wonder what could have been. What should have been if my life didn't seem determined to screw me out of love.

God, why is nothing ever easy?

I end up with Gloria on my lap, a song in my head, a melody emerging. I'm unaware when Rob left, but I find myself alone on my porch, the glass of whiskey forgotten, working on a song.

My first live performance in front of a crowd in fifteen years is in three days, and even though I'm excited and happy and incredulous, it doesn't taste quite as sweet as I want it to because, deep down, I know I was wrong to let Jonny walk away. I was wrong to let him. He was wrong to go. I was wrong to think I could be strong enough to forget him, to move on without him. We were both wrong to think that what we had was going to be easily forgotten or healed.

I shouldn't have touched him. Shouldn't have kissed him. Shouldn't have fucked him. Shouldn't have slept all those nights in the sand with him behind me. Shouldn't have woken up beside him, smelling him, hearing him, feeling him. Shouldn't have let him inside me, into my heart, into my head, or between my thighs. None of it. Because all I have now are a few hot memories and a gaping wound in my heart, where he should be, where he was, where he never will be.

Yeah, it's stupid. He gave me the *tingles*. That should have been the biggest and reddest of red flags. I barely know him. I spent less than a week with him. It was a little bit of sex and some intensely emotional situations.

But . . . even though it doesn't make a damn bit of sense, he's . . . *inside* me. I don't mean that in the dirty way, either. I wish I did, because *God* I miss the feel of him.

I shouldn't be in love with him, but I am.

10

New York City

Delta is everywhere I fucking go. *Mierda*, I can't escape her. That song, her voice, that video, her face. I've spent the last three days rattling around NYC like a marble in a can, lost, in a daze, trying to escape her, trying to avoid the feelings I'm fighting. Yeah, it's easy to think about not running, easy to think about staying . . . it's a lot harder to actually do. I'm fighting the urge to bolt, but I don't know what to do.

Just find her and be like, so I think I love you?

Find her . . . where? Go to Chicago and knock on a million doors?

Essentially, I'm frozen with indecision, which is fucking emasculating. I can sail a boat across the ocean alone.

I can fix an engine, I can swim like a fish, I can survive shipwrecks and hurricanes and typhoons, I can lobster, trawl, cook, hold my own in a fight, and even pilot a freighter the size of a damn village, but one woman has brought me to this . . . frozen with indecision.

It's embarrassing.

Worse yet, the more I think about her, the more I try to convince myself to forget her and move on, which leads me to trying to figure out why I can't get her out of my head. It's an obsession. All I do all day is go around and around in circles, telling myself to forget her, it wasn't anything real so just move on you stupid *puta* . . . and then I get sucked into thinking about her. Her eyes, her skin, her smell. The way she touched me. The way she felt. The sound of her voice whispering, or talking, or singing. God, the way she sang. The sight of her in the light of the bonfire, a guitar on her lap, eyes closed, sorrow on her face, singing a haunting song in that hypnotic voice. She packs so much expression into the way she sings, each note becomes its own emotion, each layer of her voice its own distinct entity. I want to hear her sing again. I want her to sing to me. I want . . . fuck, I just want *her*.

But it's so dumb. *Mierda*, I've gone in circles a trillion times, trying to talk myself out of the way I feel.

You can't fall in love that fast, I tell myself.

Love isn't real anyway, I tell myself.

It was incredible sex with a gorgeous woman and

that's all it was, I tell myself.

It wasn't just *incredible* sex, though, is the problem. It was so much more than that. *Jesus Cristo*, so much more. More than the slide of skin, more than the touch, the kiss, the orgasm. What was it? I don't know, I can't put it into words even in my own head. I've tried.

If I'm going to stay on land, I need to find work. So I hit up a temp agency and look for a short-term gig to get my feet wet in the dry-land employment world, and to get my mind off Delta.

My first job is working security at a concert venue. I go through the orientation, get the shirt and headset and briefing. I'm the newest guy, so I'm paired with a full-time security guard and told to walk the perimeter with him, keep people from doing stupid shit, basically. Seems easy enough, and I'm thrown in right away.

I don't have time to ask who's playing before I'm monitoring the still-empty stadium as the first people begin streaming in through the doors. There's a manic bustle on stage as the crew finishes last minute setup, sound goes through last second checks, and lighting goes through theirs.

I stay toward the back, stick with my partner, and do my best to look intimidating. It's boring, for the most part, especially for the first hour, with people filing in. There's country music playing over the house speakers, so I suspect the main draw is a country artist. I could ask my partner, but he speaks with an African dialect and has very little English, and doesn't seem inclined to chat anyway, so I don't bother. Not like it matters, anyway.

The venue is half-full when there's some commotion on stage, a tech testing the mic one last time, a single mic stand at the very front of the stage, by itself. The tech leaves, and the lights go down. Silence, expectant, as the audience waits to see who will come out.

At this point, my patrol of the perimeter has brought me to the far left of the stage, and now my partner beckons for me to follow him up the center row toward the stage. I scan the rows of people, watching for anything out of place, and so I miss the moment when the first performer comes out, but I'm alerted by the scattered applause and and a few wolf whistles.

My scan brings my gaze back to the stage, and I'm stopped dead in my tracks. I'm less than fifty feet from the stage, staring at the mic. Blinking hard, trying to clear my vision . . .

This has to be a hallucination.

Delta.

Standing at the mic, guitar hanging by the strap in front of her body. She's plugging it in, glancing down to check that the plug is seated in tight, adjusting the mic stand, and then her gaze travels to the crowd.

"Hey, y'all!" She smiles bright as the sun, and I'm blinded. "I'm Delta Martin, and I am absolutely thrilled to be here. Seriously, you don't even know what today means to me, to be on this stage, gettin' ready to play my songs for you guys, opening for freaking Miranda Lambert? Are you kidding me? Honestly? I'm still pinching myself because it still doesn't feel real. Am I real? Is this real? Let me hear you guys get real loud, just to make sure I'm really awake."

She's playing chords softly, background music for her words, and at her encouragement, the crowd howls and cheers, a deafening noise. Delta grins even more widely, playing the same few chords in a simple progression, just staring out at the crowd, her eyes shining.

"Wow. Y'all are real, huh? All right. Let's sing some songs, huh?"

She launches into a fast, upbeat, hard-driving song about drinking and forgetting who you're with, and the crowd stands up and starts clapping and stomping their feet. It's crazy catchy with an easy chorus, and halfway through the song the audience is singing along, and Delta is just beaming, glowing with joy.

She finishes the song and hangs her head, laughing, shoulders shaking, raw emotion pouring off her. "Wow, that is such a rush! I don't know how much you guys know about me other than the one song going around right now. Probably not much, I'm guessing. Don't worry, I won't tell you my life story or nothing, but I just want you to know why I'm so excited to be up here." She spins a quick story about being an eager young songwriter in Nashville, writing dozens of songs and getting nowhere, and then finally brings it around to introducing a song. "So, finally I sold a song. Y'all may have heard of it, it's a little song called 'Another Bar, Another Mic.'"

I'm absolutely frozen in place, stopped dead in my tracks. Ignoring my job, ignoring the crowd around me. Ignoring everything. I've got eyes for no one and nothing but Delta. She hasn't seen me yet, I don't think, understandably more interested in the audience, and with no reason to think I'd be here.

If she sees me . . .

Shit, if she sees me, it might throw her off, and this is her big break.

I force my eyes off her and wrench myself away. I move past my partner—don't even know his name—and I find my way to the backstage area, amid the frenetic bustle of crew members. I find a spot in the shadows where I can hide and watch.

She plays a few more raucous drinking songs, keeping the crowd moving and clapping.

The notes quaver, and Delta's shoulders lift and fall as she stares out the crowd, which I can see from here has grown to sold-out capacity.

When silence reigns, she picks out a slow, sad melody. "Changing pace here for a minute," she says. "So, ladies. This one is for you. Guys, I think you can probably relate, but I wrote this one for myself when I was having a particularly hard day, feeling sorry for myself, hating life, hating men, hating love." There's a huge wave of shrieks and whistles from the women in the crowd, and

Delta laughs and nods. "See? Y'all get it. This song is about that feeling. It's called 'Until It's Gone.'"

The song is the one she played as I was walking away.

Fuck.

I force myself to remain still, because the hurt I hear in her voice is palpable, it's as if in singing this song she's putting herself right back into that moment, feeling that pain all over again, and I want to comfort her. I want to take her in my arms and whisper soothing words to her like I did that day on the beach, when we first met.

But I don't.

I stay here, in the shadows, watching, hurting with her.

When she ends the song, there's a long moment of tense silence, and then it shatters into deafening applause, louder than ever.

She lets it go on for a moment and then strums the strings a few times, quieting the audience. "So . . . while I'm on the topic of heartbreak . . . wanna hear another sad song? I'm full of 'em, y'all. I've got a son, his name is Alex, and he's six, and he said the other day, Mom, you're *always* sad.' Which, I guess, has been true for most of my life. There's been a lot of heartbreak and a lot of sadness, which as a person kind of sucks," she says, laughing, "but as a songwriter, it's a lyrical gold-mine, know what I'm saying? So yeah, here's another one about heartbreak. This one is for all those lovers out there who have loved and lost and learned that, shit, maybe it's not so much better after all. This one is called 'Cry All Night.'"

She plays the intro and sets the melody, slow and sorrowful, and when she starts the lyrics, my throat closes.

"Dawn breaks, pink on the beach
Love sick, you're out of reach
You sat in the shadows, listening
You missed my tears, didn't see 'em glistening
I cried that night
Yeah, I cried all right

You said it won't work
I said it won't hurt
That was me lyin',
Because baby we shoulda kept tryin'
Instead you walked away, sighin'
And now I'm alone and I'm dyin'

Dawn breaks, pink on the street
Love sick, can't even eat
All night I think of you
All night I dream of you
Stay up all night, whisper your name
Stare at the ceiling, left wondering
Do you feel the same
And I cry at night
God, I cry all right

You said it won't work
I said it won't hurt
That was me lyin',
Because baby we shoulda kept tryin'
Instead you walked away, sighin'
And now I'm alone and I'm dyin'.''

I can't breathe, can't see past the blurring of my eyes. Which is stupid, because I'm a man, a Latino man at that, and I don't cry; I don't get emotional over anything, let alone a song. But here I am, clogged up for the second time in three damn days.

More wild applause as she goes through the chorus a few more times, and then finishes the song, and I see a lot of faces in the crowd feeling the lyrics.

She strums a few times, considering. "One more sad song, and then I'll go back to fun ones, is that all right?"

There's a deafening roar of approval, and Delta laughs, switching from idle strumming to playing a melody. This one is the slowest and most haunting yet, and I grit my teeth and get ready.

"'This is called 'Where Are You, Lover?''" she says, and then glances down at her strings, closing her eyes, summoning whatever it is inside her driving these wrenching, emotional songs.

"I know what they say
Can't always get it your way

You can't always get what you want
So the song goes
I wanna be in love,
Know what every other lover knows
Someone to hold, someone to kiss
Someone to fight with, someone to miss

Been down a thousand roads
Played a thousand chords
Sung a thousand songs
About a thousand wrongs
Sing about men always leavin'
Men I'll never love, and how I leave 'em
So many words, so many lines
One night stands, too many times
Get up on stage, there's only one mic
Sing my songs, only my voice
Play my guitar, only my chords
Only my strings, only my words

I know what they say
Can't always get it your way
You can't always get what you want
So the song goes
But I wanna be in love,
Know what every other lover knows
Someone to hold, someone to kiss
Someone to fight with, someone to miss

Hello life, are you listenin'
I've got one request
One thing I want, and screw the rest
Can I get another mic next to mine
Someone to write the next line
Can I get another voice, singing harmony
Sound check, mic check, play guitar with me
Long days, long roads, drive with me
Late nights and shit gigs, another set with me

I know what they say
Can't always get it your way
You can't always get what you want
So the song goes
But I wanna be in love,
Know what every other lover knows
Someone to hold me, someone to kiss
Someone to fight with, someone to miss

Where are you, lover
Can you hear me
Come closer, baby, wanna feel you near me
This bed is too big without you
Life is too short, can't live without you
Where are you, lover
I'm beggin' you please
Don't stay gone, don't be long
I'm writing this song, and maybe I'm wrong

But what we had, baby,
Maybe it's meant to be
Maybe you're meant for me
Maybe this love isn't just fiction
I want you, I need you, my fingers are itchin'
Need to touch you, need to feel you

So don't stay gone, don't be long
I'm writing this song, and maybe I'm wrong
But what we had baby,
Maybe it's meant to be
Maybe you're meant for me

I know what they say
Can't always get it your way
You can't always get what you want
So the song goes
But I wanna be in love,
Know what every other lover knows
Someone to hold me, someone to kiss
Someone to fight with, someone to miss . . ."

I know I said this already about the song of hers I heard on the radio, but I really truly mean it just as deeply now, if not more so: I'm gutted. She poured herself into that song, and as she plays the last chorus through, she lets the strings hum into silence and grips the mic in both hands and belts out the chorus, eyes closed, her entire body straining toward the mic stand just singing those last two lines through over and over again, until she finally draws out the last note into a wordless wail that fills the entire venue with her soul-shuddering emotion.

There's total silence for what feels like an eternity.

And, at that moment, she glances off-stage. I thought I was safe in the shadows, but she sees me. She sees me.

She blinks several times, peering at me, as if trying to figure out if she's really seeing what she thinks she's seeing. I step backward, but that only puts me into a pool of light from an exit sign, illuminating me. When she finally realizes it truly is me, her head droops, and she clings to the mic stand as if it's all that's holding her up.

She turns away from me, with visible effort, returning her attention to the crowd. The tableau, her seeing me, it happened in a split-second; it was nothing but a moment in the silence of the audience processing the song she just sang. And then they go nuts, and Delta glances back at me. Her expression is so fraught with emotion I don't really know how to decipher everything she's clearly feeling.

She leans subtly in my direction, as if her body wants to go to me, and I feel myself straining for her. I want to go to her. I don't want her to be heartbroken any more. I don't want her to feel such sadness, such sorrow. I don't want her to feel the ache of loneliness.

I know what that feels like, because I've felt it my

whole life, too. I've spent my life fleeing from it. My entire life has been spent literally attempting to sail away from my loneliness.

The night Christian handed me that box, I'd been trying to drown the loneliness in the bottom of a bottle of tequila. It only made me maudlin and then angry. That has been my life: sail away from my feelings, and when I hit land, get drunk and try to bury my loneliness under the liquor, try to fuck it out with easy women. None of it has ever worked.

The ache of emptiness inside, it doesn't matter how far I go, I'll never escape it.

Maybe I never will.

But . . . maybe . . . maybe I can help Delta escape hers. Maybe with her, I'll learn to let go of it all. Learn how to . . . live, I suppose. How to live a life without running from everything I am, from what I really want.

Delta stares at the crowd as they quiet, finally subsiding into silence. "All right, y'all, I've got one more song for you. This one is called 'Shouldn't Be In Love.'" She laughs, a sad huff, glances at me. "Anyone ever felt like that? The feeling where you . . . you fell in love with someone despite promising yourself you weren't going to? We can't help falling in love, but when life makes it impossible to actually be with that person, and you're in love with them anyway, it hurts, you know?"

She plays her guitar softly, quietly, staring at the floor between her feet.

I can't help staring at her, watching her. God, she's so beautiful. She's wearing a blue sundress with a leather belt cinched around her middle; the deep indigo of the dress matches the vivid blue of her eyes and her long black hair is loose around her shoulders, twisted into loose curls.

God, how did I manage to walk away from her that night on the beach? How did I do it? I don't think I can do it again. She belongs in my arms. I don't care where I have to go, what I have to do, I can't walk away from her again.

Delta glances at me again, and our eyes meet. And then she turns her attention to the crowd. "This song is for you, Jonny," she says with one last look at me.

"Shouldn't be in love, but baby I am
I know it's crazy, but I don't give a damn
God you're like a drug, I'm addicted
I want you, but I'm conflicted
Shouldn't let myself have you,
But whenever I'm near you I come unglued
Can't keep it in, can't stay subdued

Shouldn't be in love, but baby I am
I know it's crazy, but I don't give a damn
Shouldn't want you near me
But you're inside me, can you hear me
I'm praying you need me, baby say you do

I'm lying in bed, dreaming of you
Cuz I remember you moving, gliding
Can't get over you, baby I'm trying
Why can't I have you, why's it have to be so
    complicated
The love I feel hasn't faded

Shouldn't be in love, but baby I am
I know it's crazy, but I don't give a damn
I feel you inside me
Don't mean it like that, but I wish it were true
Truth is, baby, I need you
I'm missing you and this wishing you were here, it's
    killing me
I hate each day without you, when I should be happy
I'm getting what I wanted, but you're not here and
    I'm dying
Moving on shouldn't be so hard, but I'm trying
It's not working, my heart is hurting
Getting over you, thought it'd be a sure thing

I shouldn't be in love, but baby I am
I know it's crazy, but I don't give a damn
Loving you is crazy but baby I can't shake it
It's gonna get me hurt, but I can't fake it
So many days without, I can't take it
I shouldn't be in love, but I am
I know it's crazy, but I don't give a damn."

She goes through the last stanza a few more times, glancing at me now and again, and her eyes plead with me. The deep blue of her eyes calls me, speaks to me. I hear her voice, but I also hear what she's not saying.

Love me back, she's begging.

The crowd howls wildly, clapping, whistling. Every seat is filled, and they're all focused on Delta, cheering her on, and she's waving at them, lifting her guitar up by the neck.

"I can't thank you guys enough. This has been the most amazing night of my life. To be here, to be able to play for you has been an absolute privilege." She waves one last time to thunderous applause. "Have a good night, and thank you!"

And then she's striding off stage, guitar hanging by the strap behind her back. She's on her way to becoming the star she always should have been, and her life is going to be crazy, and I have no idea what to do, or where to go, but I know I can't leave her again. My feet are rooted to the floor, and now that she's here . . . I can't resist her.

I know it's crazy, but I don't give a damn, she sang.

She stops right in front of me, just off-stage, chin lifted. Around us, people swirl and bustle, coiling cords, and bringing out a rack of guitars. The stage crew is getting ready for the next opening act, but I'm barely aware of them.

All I see is Delta.

A long moment of silence as we just stare at each other.

"Jonny, I—" she starts.

My hands curl around her waist, pulling her up against me. Her breasts press against my chest, her thighs brush mine, her hands flutter between us, and then she reaches up to cup my face as I lean down, slanting my lips over hers. I kiss her. She tastes like lip balm and whiskey, smells like perfume, and feels like the home I've never had.

I can hear whistles and cheers from the people backstage, but I ignore them.

Delta's hands slide into my hair, and she lifts up on her toes, deepening the kiss, pulling me closer. Desperation sears through me, desperation like I've never felt in my life. I've tasted her, I've felt her, and I've been without her. I can't be without her any longer.

Delta breaks the kiss, panting. "Oh my God." She's momentarily flustered but then she says firmly, "Come with me."

And with that she takes me by the hand and leads me to her dressing room.

As we work our way through the labyrinth of the theater, my emotions are all over the place. I've had the most important moment of my life and then I find Jonny waiting for me backstage.

There are people everywhere, but somehow, in the crowd, Rob finds me.

"Delta, honey, you were goddamned magnificent! I swear, if opening acts could do encores, you'd be back out there right now!" Rob glances at me, and then at Jonny, and grins. "Ahh . . . it all makes sense, now." He grabs me by the shoulders and pushes me gently. "Go, baby, go! Take this boy to your dressing room."

I lead Jonny to my little dressing room, close the door behind us, lock it, and stand facing him, trying to catch my breath at the sight of him.

"Jonny, what are you doing here?" I finally ask.

"I had to come to New York to get a new passport and stuff, and once I did that I . . . I couldn't leave. If I left the States, I'd be leaving you. I'd be getting on a boat and sailing away from you. I couldn't do it."

"You . . . you couldn't?" The fragile tendril of hope in my voice stabs me like a knife; I don't want to hope. Hope hurts too much.

"And then I heard your song on the radio, and I . . . God, Delta, that song killed me."

I sigh shakily, "It wasn't supposed to feel like this, Jonny."

"No, it wasn't."

"I thought I could do it, I thought I could let you go," I whisper, resting my forehead against his. "I thought I could get over you. It's only been a month—but being apart from you hurts worse than ever."

"How do you mean?"

"Being alone again," I whisper, my lips against his. "Missing you. Wanting you."

"But I'm here now."

I pull back far enough to look him full in the face. "Yeah, but for how long?" Jonny tries to pull me close again, but I move farther away, trying to escape. "What's changed between us in the last few weeks? Our lives *still* don't fit together, Jonny."

"That may be true, but"—he tugs me back to him— "I don't think I can let you go again."

"You never let me go—you walked away."

"Yeah, I did, but we agreed there was no other choice."

I sigh and shake my head. "It's more impossible than ever, actually. I have a national tour happening. Interviews, talk shows. It's all blowing up for me, Jonny, and I've got Alex. I don't know how I'm going to manage it all, how I'm going to take care of Alex and make this work."

"Nothing is impossible," Jonny says, looking into my eyes. "It can work. People do it all the time."

"How?" I shake my head. "I can't see how I can manage Alex, and these new career opportunities, *and* a love life."

"What about the song you just sang to me, Delta? *Shouldn't be in love, but I am, crazy but I don't give a damn.* That's what you said."

"It's just a song," I say, looking anywhere but at Jonny.

He touches my chin and tilts my face so I'm looking at him. "It's not just a song, Delta. I know it, and you know it. It's way more than that."

"I can't do this with you right now, Jonny. Not here, not now." I let out a shuddering sigh and push past him to sit on the small leather couch shoved up against one wall of this tiny dressing room.

In the relative quiet, I break down. What should have been the happiest day of my life has gone to shit. I being to sob and I can't stop.

It's all too much.

"Delta."

I cover my face with both hands. "How can this be the best day of my life and the worst at the same time?" I ask.

"Honestly, Delta, I didn't know you'd be here when I took this job. I didn't plan this. I'm sorry I ruined your day." I see the confusion and sadness in his eyes, and he looks away, running his fingers through his hair.

I laugh. "Believe it or not, you didn't ruin it, Jonny."

"Sure seems like I did if you're in here sobbing when you should be out there celebrating."

I try to pull myself together, sucking in deep breaths and letting them out slowly, shakily. Finally, I look at him, my eyes wet and shining with tears. "You mix me up so bad."

"How do I mix you up?"

I shrug. "You just . . ." I sigh deeply. "Whenever you're close to me like this, I feel as if anything's possible. Just being around you makes everything feel—"

"Better?" he says.

"Yeah, better. You make me feel *alive*, Jonny." I want to touch him, but I'm afraid. I don't know what to do with my hands. "I've been . . . floating, for so long, just surviving. Getting through each day, taking care of Alex. Get laid occasionally, get drunk alone at home after work sometimes. Pathetic and lonely, that's how I'd describe my life. And now, being near you, I feel like . . . God, I don't even know how to describe it. It feels like life has some kind of meaning, even though nothing is different, except you're near me. And I . . . I *want* that feeling, Jonny. I want it all the time."

"Delta, I—I want that too."

"But *how*, Jonny?" I shake my head. "I don't see how I can have that without stealing your sealskin, and I'm *not* going to do that."

Jonny frowns at me, confused. "Sealkskin? What are you talking about?"

"Remember Christian's short story for Ava?"

"Oh yeah, that." He moves so he's looking directly at me. "I'm not a selkie, Delta, and I'm not Christian. So . . . if I choose to stay, that's not you stealing anything, or forcing me to stay, or tricking me. It would be a choice I make for my own reasons."

"You're a sailor, you sail—that's what you said to me."

"I know what I said."

I'm puzzled. "Are you suddenly not a sailor anymore?"

"I don't know what I am anymore," he says. "Except . . . I'm falling in love with you."

"Goddammit, Jonny." I shudder, trying to keep the tears at bay. "You can't say that to me."

"Why not? It's the truth."

"Because I want that so fucking bad!" I stand and pace past Jonny, my guitar slinging around to bump against my butt. "I've never had anyone, and I—I want *you*! I want to be with you. There, I said it."

"Okay, so—"

"But I couldn't handle it if you changed your mind. What if you settle for life with me, on land, and discover you hate it. What then? And, besides, what would you do? How would it work?"

"I don't know!" he shouts and then repeats it more quietly. "I don't know, Delta. I don't have that figured out. I only know I've been going crazy the last few weeks, working myself to exhaustion trying not to think about you, trying to convince myself I don't fucking miss you. Then I heard that *damn* song of yours on the radio, and then I kept hearing it everywhere I fucking went, and each time I hear it it fucking kills me!

"I didn't want to walk away, but I thought it was for the best, for you and for me both. I thought it was what I was supposed to do. We talked about it—we agreed. But try telling that to my fucking stupid heart."

He's been pacing as he speaks, but now he turns and stands right in front of me. His hands grip my waist and stares hard into my eyes. "I don't know what it would look like, or how it would work," he says. "All I know, Delta, is I want it. I want you. I want *us*."

"Don't tease me, Jonny. Don't make me want something I can't have." I stare at him, my eyes wet with unshed tears.

A single tear trickles down my cheek, and he brushes

it away with his thumb. "I'm not teasing, Delta. I don't know if you've noticed, but I'm not exactly a laugh-a-minute sort of guy."

"I can't handle more disappointment, Jonny. I can't take any more heartbreak. I stopped trying to care about anyone except Alex a long time ago. I'm not sure I even know how to . . ." I trail off, laughing. "It's easy to write about this in a song, easy to sing about, but to honestly talk about . . . love for myself? It's fucking hard."

"I know what you mean," he says. "I've never been in love before, never stuck around any one place long enough to let anything like that happen. Nobody has ever . . . meant anything to me until I met you. So I have to be honest, and I really don't know what the hell I'm doing."

"Same here." I lean against his solid form, and let him hold me as I let out a long breath. "If neither of us has had a real relationship before . . . where do we start?"

He laughs. "You're asking me? I have no fuckin' idea, babe, I just know I want it."

"Just . . . don't break my heart, Jonny," I whisper. "I won't survive it, and I have to survive for Alex."

"Delta, listen—I'm from Latin America, and if you know anything about our culture, as men we aren't really big on *mierda* like talking about our emotions, or being in touch with 'em. I grew up taking care of my family, with no real father figure. I've always been alone, kept my own company and kept my own counsel. Emotions are hard for me. To be honest, I've spent most of my life avoiding the way I feel about anyone or anything. So it's hard for me to admit this, is what I'm saying, but . . . the way I feel about you fuckin' scares the shit out of me. I don't know how to deal with it." He caresses my cheek with my thumb. "You have this . . . power over me, honey. You could fuckin' wreck me. You could . . . you could destroy me. The way I feel, it's . . . I wouldn't know what to do *without* you. God knows I've tried, and I've frozen. That's why I'm here, at this concert, working security. I had to fuckin' *do* something, because I couldn't make myself leave. I'd think about getting a berth on a ship, and I'd freeze up. I couldn't do it. Because you were here. If I left the States, I'd be leaving you for good, and I couldn't do it. And now you're here, I've got you in my arms again, and I fuckin' . . . I can't handle losing you again. Walking away the first time damn near gutted me, and there ain't no way I could do it again. So if . . . if you and me ain't gonna work, I . . . I don't know . . . I don't know what I'll do."

I blink at him, fresh tears sliding down my face. "Oh, Jonny."

"What?"

I palm his cheek. "I . . . I fucking love you, that's what."

"You do?"

"Yes, you *loco* man, I do."

And then he kisses me.

Slowly, deeply. Taking his time, relishing the feel of my lips pressing against me.

I try to hold back my need . . . and fail. My attempts to keep this to just a kiss are ruined by the way I cling to him. I grab his shirt and lift up on my toes; my heart is hammering and I can feel his hard cock behind his zipper. His hands go to my backside, palming my ass. I can't help myself, letting out a deep moan at his hands fierce grip.

"God, Jonny," I murmur. "I need you."

"You can't say shit like that to me," he whispers to me.

"Why?"

"Because I'm barely controlling myself right now."

I look at him, and I know my eyes are as wild as I feel. Moments pass, my eyes are on his, and then his hands claw into the meat of my ass and my hips press hard against his throbbing erection, my breasts flattening against his chest. Both of us are breathing hard, resisting, needing, desire battling against the fact that we're in public.

Delta leaps onto me, wrapping her legs around me, clinging to my neck and shoulders. She kisses me, and the ferocity of her kiss is a drug, sending euphoria through me, sending me to heaven and undercutting the last of my self-control. I moan as her tongue slips into my mouth, and I walk with her to the wall.

I pin her spine to the wall and delve deeper into the kiss. She whimpers, and her hips swivel, grinding into me. She releases her legs and slides down her feet, my hands buried in the soft cotton of her dress, gathering it in my fist and lifting it. I hold the hem of the dress up around her waist with one hand, and trace the damp seam of her pussy over the silk of her underwear with the other.

She whimpers again, pressing into my touch. I slide a finger between the gusset and her flesh, and find her clit, damp with desire and hard. A few slow circling touches and she's grinding into my finger and gasping as I kiss her. Delta's hands are fumbling for me, bunching in my shirt and sliding under the hem to palm my stomach.

I'm seconds from ripping her underwear off and taking her right now. Instead, I break the kiss and slip my finger out.

She gasps and stares at me. "Jonny . . . why the fuck did you stop?"

"We shouldn't do this here, Delta," I growl. "Any more, and I'm not gonna be able to stop myself."

She blinks and something shifts in her gaze. Wildness and ferocity blossom into primal need.

With a shimmy of her hips, Delta lowers the tiny blue thong she's wearing and tosses it onto the floor. She lifts it with her toe, snags it with her finger, and stuffs it into the back pocket of my jeans.

"Who asked you to stop?" she asks, reaching for my belt buckle. "I sure as fuck didn't."

"Delta . . ." I breathe.

"Jonny," she says back.

She stares up at me, loosening the tension on my belt and unthreading it.

"Here?" I ask.

She unbuttons my jeans, lowers the zipper. "Here. Now."

"This is crazy."

She reaches in and fists my erection, baring me. "First time was on a beach at sunrise, a few days after a hurricane. Second time might as well be in my dressing room after a gig, Everything about us is crazy."

I tug the neckline of her dress, exposing her tits. I bend to kiss them, licking her nipples, moaning at the taste of her skin. "*Mierda*, Delta. You taste so good."

She clings to my neck and leaps into my arms again, wrapping her thighs around my waist. "I'm gonna feel even better, once you're inside me."

I growl at the slippery warm silk of her thighs against my bare waist, at the wet warmth of her pussy against my erection. Moan at the sudden onslaught of her kiss, the wild hunger of her mouth on mine, which I return and match with an urgency of my own.

She leans back, palms my jaw. "I need you inside me, Jonny."

Reaching between us, she guides me to her entrance, fits me inside her, and sinks down around me; we both moan breathlessly.

I pin her against the wall, my hands on her ass, holding her up, flexing my hips to slide deeper. "You feel better than you did the first time," I say.

"Feels like being home," Delta mumbles. "Your cock inside me . . . you kissing me . . . it's home."

"Never had a home," I breathe.

"You do now," Delta says, nipping kisses to my jaw

as I move inside her; her kisses graze across my mouth and she bites my lower lip, then kisses me, softly, quickly. "Me, I'm your home."

We move in synch as I kiss her and thrust into her, holding her, feeling her arms surround me and her pussy tightening around me. Our breathing is matched, intensity ratcheting to a frenetic frenzy. I can't hold back, can't wait, and don't try. She's there with me, gasping and groaning.

"Jonny, shit . . . I'm gonna come," she gasps. "Come with me. Come inside me," she shrieks.

"I am, Delta, I'm coming, *mierda*, Delta . . ." I moan, then I'm coming and she's coming with me, exploding around me, clinging to me fiercely and biting her lip to quiet her desperate shrieks. *"Te amo, eres encantador mi amor . . ."* and I lose track of what I'm saying, unaware of whether I'm speaking Spanish or English, or a mixture of both. I know I'm telling her I love her again and again.

Finally, Delta lifts up to slide me out of her and regains her feet, and I hold on to her, clutching her against my chest, both of us gasping for breath.

After a few moments, neither of us totally put together or in control of our breathing, we hear a knock at the door.

"Delta? You in there, girl?" A gruff male voice calls.

She laughs and straightens her dress, tugging and stuffing and shimmying until she's presentable, combing her fingers through her hair. "I'm here, Rob," she says as she opens the door.

"Ah, right. Sorry to interrupt," he says, a little sheepishly.

Delta wraps an arm around my waist. "I needed a few minutes with Jonny."

Rob's gaze is knowing. "You two figure things out?"

She shrugs. "We're . . . still working on it, but getting there."

"Well, you'll have to work on it later, because Miranda is asking for you to join her on a few songs," Rob says. "So, you know, freshen up a bit and get your ass on stage."

Delta blinks. "She's . . . what?"

"Miranda is asking for you to go out there and play with her," Rob says. "Like, *now*."

Delta stares back blankly. "She is?"

Rob claps his hands, suddenly, loudly. "Yes! Now get out there, girl! Don't make the woman ask twice."

Delta takes a quick peek in the mirror, exclaiming, "Holy shit! Holy shit I just need to use the bathroom real quick, and then I'm out there. Five minutes—no, less than that! Two minutes!"

She pauses, glancing back at me. "Jonny, I—"

"*Mujer loca!*" I cut over her, waving her away. "Go!"

She vanishes through the doorway, and I watch her leave. Rob stays back, and faces me once Delta is gone. "She's been a mess about you, son."

"I've been a mess about her."

He gestures toward the entrance to the stage. "This is her big break. Don't fuck it up for her."

"No way."

He eyes me, the security shirt, the switched off two-way radio. "You know, she could use a full time body-guard. Things are about to get crazy for her."

"Whatever I gotta do, I'll do," I say. "I'm just not leaving her again. If you want me to head up her security team, I'm your man."

He nods. "You're hired, then. First job is to make sure she gets on stage ASAP. Go!"

I find her exiting a bathroom, her hair touched up, makeup fixed. "Guess I'm your full-time security guy now."

She smiles. "I feel safer already." She touches her hair. "I look okay?"

I laugh. "You look incredible."

She leans close. "Do I look like I just got fucked?"

"Maybe a little," I tease. "Kidding. No, you look perfect."

She blows out a breath. "The only thing bigger for me than opening for Miranda is playing with her. This is huge, Jonny."

I gently guide her to the wings of the stage, where the star of the show is playing a slow, sad song about a tin man. "Go, baby. Be awesome."

She eyes me, laughing. "Nothing like going out to perform with one of the biggest stars in country music

. . . with come dripping down my thigh."

"I thought you cleaned up."

"I did, but . . . there was a lot."

"Sorry."

She lifts up, kisses me. "Don't be—I'm not. And you've still got my thong in your pocket, you know."

"Want it back?"

She laughs again. "Hell no." She shakes her hands, bounces on her toes. "Wish me luck."

"You don't need luck, babe, you got talent. You're gonna kill it."

She takes a few steps onto the stage, and when the crowd sees her they cheer wildly.

"Hey!" I call out, and she turns to glance at me, walking backward. "I love you."

She grins ear to ear, but there's no time for anything else, because a guitar tech is handing Delta a guitar and Miranda is welcoming her on stage.

"I was wondering when you'd find your way back on stage," Miranda teases.

"Sorry, I had . . . a situation."

"Is that a situation of the tall, dark, and handsome variety?"

Delta laughs, ducking her head. "Maybe?"

"That there is a good-lookin' situation," Miranda says glancing at me, laughing, and then turns to Delta again. She strums a chord then another one. "I saw a video online of you doing 'Another Bar, Another Mic,' looked like a video someone had taken with a cell phone or something. I wanted you on this tour with me based on that video. I've always loved that song, and I feel like you and me should give it a try."

"Sounds good to me," Delta replies, to loud cheering.

And then they're off, playing that song. The last time I heard it, I was on the beach, about to walk away from Delta. Things are . . . a little different, this time around.

P laying with Miranda is . . . beyond a dream come true. I've idolized her for years and have followed her career every step of the way. And now I'm onstage with her? Doing a duet of my song with her? It's crazy. We play two more songs together, and then I get the signal to get off stage, but before I do, Miranda hugs me.

"Go get him," she whispers.

"I already did," I whisper back, giggling. "That's why I took so long getting out here."

Miranda laughs as I stride off stage, and then the lights come down and a tech is taking her guitar, and another one is taking mine, and the crowd is howling, cheering as Miranda plugs me one more time.

I've only got eyes for Jonny, though, and as I exit the

stage I see that Alex and Ava are standing beside him.

I got them tickets for the show, and I haven't seen them since lunchtime. Somehow they found their way backstage and bumped into Jonny. Ava's got a confused look on her face, but Alex is taking it in stride, the way six-year-olds tend to do; he and Jonny are talking like old friends.

Seeing my happy face, Ava hugs me and simply says, "You deserve this, honey, all of it."

"Hey, Mommy!" Alex yells. "I made a new friend. His name is Jonny."

I smile at Jonny. "Well, hi, there, Jonny."

He grins back. "Hi there, Delta."

Alex is watching us, head bobbing back and forth like he's watching a tennis match, clearly knowing something is weird, but he can't figure it out. "Can we go now?"

I laugh and nod, and lead us all out of the backstage area. We reach my dressing room and Ava excuses herself to go to the ladies' room. I take seat on the couch and pull Alex down next to me. "So, did you like the show?"

"I loved it," Alex exclaims. "One of the guys showed me some of the guitars, and a lady let me and Aunt Ava take *anything* we wanted from the snack table . . . I took M&M's"

I smile at my precious little boy and ask, "How would you feel about Jonny being with us on the tour? Like, all the time."

Alex eyes Jonny. "Why?"

"Um. Because . . ." I struggle for an answer, not sure how much to tell him.

"Are you guys in love?" Alex asks.

I laugh, because Alex never ceases to surprise me. "Can't put anything past you, can I, kiddo?"

He moves to climb onto my lap. "So now you won't be sad anymore?"

"No, buddy, I sure won't."

He leans against my chest. "That's good." Another pause. "I still don't think I need a tutor."

"We're not talking about this again, Alex," I say. "You're *getting* a tutor."

"That's stupid." He glances at Jonny. "You're not the tutor, are you?"

Jonny laughs. "No way. Only thing I could teach you is Spanish, and maybe how to tie really good knots."

"I can tie my shoes, and I know some bad words in Spanish. I learned them from Miguel, at school, back in Chicago."

"Well, I don't think your Mom would appreciate it if I taught you bad words."

"No, I wouldn't." She taps Alex on the nose.

Ava returns and smiles—she caught the last of the conversation between us.

"Honey, I want you to go with Auntie Ava. I need to talk to Jonny alone for a minute."

"Are you guys gonna do sex?" he asks.

I splutter. "Alex Martin, where in the world did you

hear that?"

He shrugs. "School."

I sigh. "Sounds like you learned a lot of not so good stuff at that school."

He nods seriously. "Yeah, maybe. That's why I don't think a tutor is a good idea. I wouldn't learn bad stuff from PBS, now would I?"

I can't help but laugh. "Nice try. Now, go. Maybe Auntie Ava will put on a movie for you in the tour bus."

After they leave, I lock the door behind me, something Jonny doesn't miss.

"Need to talk to me alone, huh?" he asks, grinning.

I shrug, and point at the couch. "Privacy and horizontal surfaces are going to be in short supply for a while, I think," I say. "I'm not quite ready to have you move into my room on the bus just yet. I want to introduce our relationship to Alex gradually. He's never seen me with anyone."

He nods his head as I sit on the couch beside him. "I totally get that."

I eye him cautiously. "Are you sure you're up for everything a relationship with me entails? I mean, even Alex is a lot to adjust to. I'll need help with him, and he'll bond with you, and I don't want to do that if . . . if things aren't going to work out."

Jonny pulls me onto his lap, so I'm sitting sideways across his thighs. "Babe, it's gonna work out. It may not always be easy, and there may be hiccups, but we're gonna figure it out. We'll take it slow."

I pull at his belt buckle. "The only thing I want to take slow is being open about things in front of Alex," I say. "It's a little late to take our relationship itself slowly."

"How about I take you slowly?" he asks.

"I like that idea."

Since the door is locked, I stand up and remove my dress and bra, and then sink to my knees in front of him and tug his boots, socks, and jeans off, and then his shirt.

"This is the second time we've had a door to lock," I say, "and the first time was kind of rushed. I want to see you naked."

"This is the first time we've been together without having to worry about being interrupted," he says.

I'm on my knees between his thighs and he's hard. I can't resist the urge to take him into my mouth. He smells like sex and tastes like it, like his seed and my essence commingled. He groans as I take him to my throat, bob on him until he lets out a curse in Spanish. He pulls away and then lies down on his back on the couch, and I move astride him. I sink onto him, my breasts brushing his chest, and I groan at the feel of him inside me, filling me, stretching me. He pulls me down for a kiss, and that kiss becomes more, consuming us as we move together, my hips grinding against his, the thick hardness of his cock sliding and slipping, hitting me just right, bringing me to the brink within seconds. And then I'm falling over, screaming into the kiss, and Jonny is murmuring to me in Spanish in that way he does, repeating the same phrases over and over, which I think mean *I love you*, and *you're so beautiful*, and *you feel so good*, and *God, please don't stop*; I'm not exactly super fluent in Spanish, though, so they could be *oh yeah fuck me harder*, and *ride that dick, sexy mama*. You never know.

I cling to his neck and ride him through my first orgasm, and he holds out and I touch myself to get a second, and then he's moaning and growling, and I squeeze around him, palm his face and meet his gaze as he moves in me with increasing desperation, until he's pounding into me with his hands grasping my hips to yank me down onto him, and I'm whimpering and he's saying *te amo, te amo, te amo* over and over and over again, and then I feel him unleash inside me, a wet hot flood filling me, and I whisper that phrase back to him: *te amo te amo te amo*, so we're chanting it unison as I come around him a third time as he shatters inside me.

The intensity of it, of knowing this is real, that we're going to be together, that he's going to be on the tour with me, overwhelms me. I have this vision of us, him and me and Alex, together.

A family.

Tears slide down my cheeks as I fight for breath, and Jonny sees them. He doesn't ask, he knows what they mean.

"It's always been me and Alex. You and me—*us*—we . . . we could be a family." Then panic shoots through me. "Shit, shit. I don't want to scare you away, I just . . ."

He touches my mouth with two fingers, silencing me. "You can't scare me away. Not with that, not with anything." He tilts my chin so I'm looking at him. "We *are* a family, Delta. You, Alex, and me. We'll take it slow and we'll do it right, but we'll be a family."

"You're sure that's what you want?"

"More than anything. I've been running from home and from family for damn near thirty years, Delta." He smiles at me. "I'm ready. I'm done running. I *want* home and family, babe, and I want it with you and Alex."

I snuggle closer to him, more content than I've ever been, wrapped up in his arms.

On the tour bus between New York and Philadelphia: the next day

Alex is taking a rare nap and Jonny is in the Suburban with Rob and some of the guitar techs, following behind the bus, so it's just me and Ava on the bus. We're sitting at the little table near the kitchenette, and Ava is clearly chewing on something, trying to figure out how to say it.

Eventually, after idle small talk, I poke her on the shoulder. "Out with it, Ava."

"Out with what?"

I snort. "Whatever it is that's eating you."

She sighs, tracing patterns on the tabletop with her fingertip. "I . . . I'm going crazy."

"You've always been crazy, Ava. You'll have to be more specific."

She sniffles. "It's almost two months since Christian—since he—since . . ." She shakes her head, unable to finish the thought. "I just . . . I can't take it anymore."

"Oh, honey," I say, shifting closer to her. "I'm sorry. I'm so, so sorry. I can't imagine what it must be like."

She shakes her head. "You don't get it. I've tried to come to terms with the fact that he's gone, but . . . I . . . I have this feeling, Delta." She looks up, meets my gaze, and she's crying. "He's out there."

"Ava, you heard what Jonny said. That . . . it's not really possible. How could he have survived a storm like that?"

"HE'S ALIVE!" she shouts, slamming her hand on the tabletop then says it again more quietly. "He's alive. I know it. I *know* it. He's out there. He's stuck, so he can't come back, or something. I don't know. I just . . . I know this sounds crazy, but I *feel* it. I feel it in my bones, in my gut, in my blood."

"So . . . what are you going to do?"

She shakes her head. "I don't know. But I have to do something. I have to look for him. I have to."

"Ava, that's crazy. Where would you even start?"

She shrugs. "I don't know." Her gaze goes to mine, and I see the determination, the hardness that says she won't back down. "I don't know. I just know I have to look. He's out there, and he needs me. I lost Henry, I can't lose Christian, too. He's alive, and he needs me, and I'm going to find him."

"Talk to Jonny. He might have some ideas." I pause. "I love you, Ava, you know that, right? So I feel like I have to say, as your big sister, that this is crazy. Even if he is alive, he could be literally anywhere."

"I know." She nods, sniffling. "I know. I don't care. I'll look as long as it takes. I just . . . I *know* he's alive out there. I don't know how else to explain it. I know it as surely as I know my own name—Christian is alive."

"Crazier things have happened, I guess."

She nods, hesitating, and looks at me. "I already talked to Jonny, actually, and he told me where to find his friend Dominic, down in Charleston. So I called Dominic yesterday, and he's going to take me out with him. He's crossing the Atlantic, and I'm going with him. He knows lots of fishermen and boat captains and harbormasters, so he's going to help me look for Christian."

"So you do have a plan of some kind, then?"

"The start of one, yes," she says. "I . . . I don't want to leave you. Not now, not with everything that's going on with you."

I smile at her. "Ava, I'm fine. I have Jonny. And Rob."

"Jonny is amazing, and Rob is pretty cool too." Ava sniffles again. "I'm happy for you, and proud of you, you know."

I wrap her up in a hug. "Thanks." I pull away and eye Ava. "You hate fishing boats, and you hate the open ocean."

She nods, laughing. "I know. But . . . it's Christian," she says with a shrug as if that explains it.

Which, it does. Jonny and I have only been officially together for a day, but I'm already starting to get it. If something happened to Jonny, I'd probably go crazy too. And if I thought he was alive out there somewhere, needing me? I'd do anything to find him. And that's after *one day*; Ava has loved Christian for ten years. Multiply what I'm feeling by ten years' worth of days . . .

I shiver and shudder, thinking about it, trying to imagine loving Jonny that much.

"You have to go, Ava." I tighten the hug, squeezing her.

"You understand?"

"It's Christian," I say, as if that explains it.

She sniffles, and it turns to tears again. "Exactly. It's Christian."

"You sure you'll be okay? Again, may I remind you how much you hate it out on the ocean?"

She laughs through her tears. "I have to. Maybe I'll learn to love it."

"Maybe," I say, doubtfully. "So, when do you leave?"

"I'm taking a flight from Philly to Charleston, which is where Captain Dominic is. We're leaving tomorrow."

"Holy shit, that's soon."

She nods. "I've wasted too much time already. I've always felt like he's still alive, but it's now at the point where I can't handle it any more, I can't—each moment of each day I think about him, and I picture him out there, hurt, alone, needing me, and I—I hate myself for hesitating, just because I hate the ocean. I hate the ocean, but I love him, and he needs me. So . . . I'm going."

"We'll miss you."

She puts her arms around me. "You and Jonny, you saved my life. I can't ever thank you enough."

"You're my sister, dummy, and that's just how Jonny is."

She sniffles, nodding. "He's good people. I'm glad you found him."

"I'm glad I found him, too."

We talk about our men then, and I relish this time, just me and Ava hanging out together, talking about boys, giggling over dirty stories, being sisters.

A few hours later, we reach Philadelphia, and Jonny, Alex, Ava, and I take the Suburban to the airport, with a driver hired by the label behind the wheel. Ava has a single duffle bag packed, and she has her ticket in hand, a frightened but determined expression on her face.

I leave Alex with Jonny in the Suburban at the drop-off line, and accompany Ava to the security line. She turns to me, wraps me up in a hug. "I'm scared, Delta."

"You'll be fine. Jonny is good people, and he trusts Dominic, which means he's good people, too, okay? You'll be fine."

"I know, it's just . . . I've lived in Florida my whole life. I've only traveled with Christian. This is the first time I've gone anywhere alone."

I can't help laughing. "Aww, my baby sister is all grown up."

"Shut up," she laughs, "don't be mean to me."

"I'm teasing." I squeeze her. "Just be careful, okay?"

"Being careful would mean not doing this, and I'm way past being careful."

I laugh and nod. "I know, I know." I push her toward security before I try to convince her to stay. "Go find your husband."

She waves without looking back, moving to join the security line. "I'll call you."

"You better. I love you!"

"Love you, too."

She's in the security line, ID and boarding pass out, getting screened through, and then she's out of sight.

Back in the Suburban, Jonny wraps his arm around my shoulders as we drive back. "She'll find him. Dominic is a good man, and he knows a lot of people all over the world. If anyone can find him, he can."

I eye him. "You wish you were out there too, don't you? Going with her to look for Christian?"

He shrugs. "Yeah, of course. He's my best friend, and . . . I spent my whole life out there." A long pause. "But my life is here, now. And if Chris is alive, which I think is *possible* if not likely, then Ava and Dom will find him."

"But you want to be out there."

He nods. "Yeah, but I want to be here more."

I rest my head on his shoulder and smile. "Good answer."

Epilogue

The day is hot. This is unsurprising, however, because all of the days have been hot, thus far. Humid, too. Lots of flies, lots of biting things.

His head hurts. This, too, is unsurprising as his head has been hurting pretty much nonstop for as long as he can remember.

Which . . . isn't much.

His mind is fuzzy, foggy. It's hard to recall things that happened earlier in the day, and impossible to remember things that happened yesterday, and further back than that? There's just . . . nothing.

Usually.

Sometimes, he gets . . . flashes. Not full memories, really, but more . . . fragments of images.

A hand: female, with candy-apple red nails, delicate purple-blue veins, a two-karat diamond solitaire ring with a platinum band on the ring finger; the hand slides down his chest, nails scraping, digging, trailing erotically down his stomach.

A sweep of short, ink black hair sprays across a pillow.

Vivid blue eyes, potent, fierce and wild.

A sailboat, a catamaran, slicing down a steep wave, the sky behind it angry, black, pregnant with a vicious storm.

Waves all around, being spun in circles and twisted and tossed like a marble in a washing machine.

A grave, a rectangle dug six feet into the soil. A tiny casket being lowered. Sunshine and black veils and tears.

Flashes of the past, but too little to cling to, each one fraught with violent emotion.

When the flashes wash through him, they paralyze him. He goes utterly still, seized by the images, squeezed by the emotions woven into the images like ivy wrapped around a tree.

He's desperate to remember.

But the harder he tries, the less he remembers. The flashes come randomly, sometimes a dozen a day, sometimes new ones, sometimes the same image repeated over and over again.

He is outside, most of the time. Sitting in an ancient, rickety wheelchair in the shade of a huge, ancient, spreading tree, and even in the shade it is oppressively hot. Gulls and terns and other shore birds make occasional appearances overhead, which means he's near the ocean.

The people around him do not speak English, and he doesn't speak their languages, one of which he's relatively certain is French. The other languages he hears are . . . well, he's not sure. African dialects, maybe? The speakers are black, most of them are medical workers, and they all seem to use their languages and dialects interchangeably. Either way, he can't make out a word, and they don't understand him, even when he can summon the ability to speak at all. There are perhaps a dozen people that come and go around him, and they see that he eats, sleeps, uses a toilet, and they regularly check his various injuries, of which there are many.

His left arm is in a cast from shoulder to fingertips, and his left leg from hip to ankle. His ribs scream in raw, excruciating agony with every breath, each movement. His right arm is in a cast, as well, but only from elbow to wrist, leaving him some use of his right hand. His head is bandaged, and it is his head they check most frequently. They shine flashlights in his eyes, hold up fingers and he knows he's supposed to tell them how many fingers there are by holding up the same number of fingers. They ask him questions, but of course he can't understand him nor they him, so the whole process seems somewhat futile to him, but they persist and he cooperates, simply because he doesn't know what else he would do.

There is one phrase that they repeat to him over and over and over again: "Comment vous appelez-vous?"

He knows this one: "What is your name?"

He doesn't know the answer, though.

There is so little he knows, so much he doesn't know.

The flashes of memory, the fragments of images, they are all he has of himself, of whatever his life was before he arrived *in this place, wherever it is, whatever it is, however he got here.*

Some days he feels like—it's so hard to put to words—he feels as if he's on a precipice, teetering on the edge, and if he just falls over he'll remember everything. Like having to sneeze, but not being able to. It's all there, but he can't quite reach it.

He's unsure how long he has been here. The days have blurred together, one day the same as the last, broken up only by the faces of the people taking care of him.

He is bored.

His skin itches underneath the casts.

His head hurts.

He wants to remember.

He NEEDS to remember.

He just . . . can't.

Then one day, a day exactly like all the others, there is a new face. A black man, middle aged, wearing a suit like a Western businessman, with kind brown eyes and straight white teeth, and large, gentle hands.

"I am James. I am a doctor. Do you understand me?" This is in thickly accented but fluent English.

"Yes, I understand you."

"Do you know what is your name?"

"I can't remember."

"Do you remember anything? How it is you came here? Where you came from? You remember anything?"

A shake of his head. "No. I have . . . pictures, images of things, but . . . nothing about who I am or where I came from."

A grave nod. "I see, I see."

"I feel like . . . I feel like I COULD remember, if I try hard enough, but . . . I just can't."

"No, no. That is not the way." James crouches, gently checks his arm, leg, and then his head, and then does the thing with the flashlight and his finger. "You suffered very much. Your head . . . this especially was badly hurt. I think your memories, they will return, but we must help them. To try too hard, this will not work. You must help the remembering, but gently."

"How?"

James rises from his crouch and walks away without a word, but with purpose in his stride, and returns a few moments later with a spiral-bound notebook and a ballpoint pen. "The pictures in your head, write them down. Tell yourself a story about the pictures. A real story, a fake story, it does not matter. Just make the little pictures into bigger ones. Tell stories about yourself. They will feel like stories, or maybe, if you are lucky, some will feel true. This is to help your memory learn to work once more. In your brain, in your head, things were hurt. We must help them heal and give them time."

"What if I never remember?"

James tsks his tongue, shakes his head. "No, no. You must not think this way. If you have the pictures, you have the memories. You will remember."

"Where am I?"

"Africa. Near Conraky, in Guinea."

"Oh." This doesn't mean much to him. "How long have I been here?"

"Over one month. Four weeks and some days."

"Where did I come from?"

*"Fishermen found you in the sea. Many injuries, no iden-
tification."* He pauses. *"One of the fishermen who found you,
I saw him just the other day. He asked about you. He told me
you said only one thing, over and over again: Ava, Ava, Ava."*
James watches the effects of his words very closely.

Ava.

Ava.

Ava.

Three letters, and with them a whirlwind of images.

The hand, candy-apple nails and delicate purple-blue
veins. The sweep of ink black hair on a crisp white pillow.
Vivid, virulently blue eyes.

His throat seizes and his muscles contract. His jaw clenches and the blue sky seems darker, and a sense of longing slams
through him, a need, a desperation.

"Ava." He whispers the name, the three letters.

Well, only two letters, really: an A, a V, and another A.
Two syllables. A breath, his teeth closing on his lower lip, and
another breath.

What does it mean? This name, the hair and the nails and
the eyes, who is she?

She is . . . everything.

What does that mean, though? He can't comprehend it all.

"This means something to you, this name?" James asks.

A heavy, slow nod. *"Yes."*

"What does it mean?"

A shrug of his shoulder. "I . . . I don't know."

"Ava . . . what does she mean to you?"

"Everything!" he shouts, sudden and loud. "She means EVERYTHING!"

James is unperturbed. "Good, very good. You have a name, an important one. Write a story about her. She is in you, somewhere. Find her."

Find her.

Find her.

James is still speaking, but the words do not register.

Eventually, he is alone once more, in the wheelchair under the shade of a tree. The notebook is on his lap, open to the first page, the pen held awkwardly in his right hand.

The white space and blue lines of the page . . . it feels familiar. Like an invitation.

He sits for a very long time, staring at the page, holding the pen, letting images and fragments of memory roll through him, letting strings of words coagulate and cohere like clumps of driftwood collecting in the lee of a tree downed in a river's current.

Sunlight drowses into evening, and the mosquitos come out and the tsetse flies and the blackflies and the other biting things, and he is wheeled back into a long, low, narrow room dimly lit by a pair of naked bulbs, with rows of cots, most of them empty, except for two still thin forms: a sick, dying man, and a woman with missing limbs and vacant, haunted eyes.

The nurses help him into his cot, and he sits with the notebook balanced on his right thigh. Stars twinkle through the window, filtered through the mosquito netting. Insects chirrup and bats flit and he even thinks perhaps he can hear a distant SSSHHHHH . . . SSSSHHHHH . . . SSSSSHHHH of waves on the shore.

It is cooler now that it is night, but it is still hot, and the air is heavy and moist with humidity, so sweat dots his forehead and upper lip all the time, and sweat trickles down his spine, and his skin itches under his casts.

Eventually, the swirling stew of images and sentences in his mind glugs sluggishly down to his fingertips and into the pen.

He grips the warm blue thin plastic tube between his forefinger, middle finger, and thumb, and touches the ballpoint tip to the first line of the first page.

In fits and starts at first, and then with increasing fervor, he begins to write.

Petrichor is heavy on the air, the thick scent of rain. Bread baking, somewhere. A dog barks. Voices chatter, a low, meaningless murmur of dissonance. Wind blows past the window, whispering and whistling; rain clatters and patters and hisses. A bell dongs rings in a church steeple, and a ship's bell answers with a jangle and clang.

Calum is restless. A wildness fills his blood, a sense of urgency rousing him to pace across his room, back and forth, back and forth, the hitch in his step and the thunk of his false leg on the wooden floor creating a rhythm: shuffle-thud . . . shuffle-thud . . . shuffle-thud.

His door creaks open, and Da appears. "Cease that infernal pacing, would you, Calum? It's enough to drive a man mad, the endless pacing."

"They should be back by now, Da." His voice is a permanent hoarse rasp.

"They will be at the dock any day now, Calum. Tis a bit of a blow, nothin' t'worry on."

"It's been a bit of a blow for a week now, and not a word from them."

"What would you have them do, Calum, fly? They're coming." More gently, now. "She'll be here, son. You'll see."

Calum pauses at the window, staring out through heavy leaded glass into the snarling storm. He shakes his head, thick, unkempt red locks falling in his face. "I have an ill foreboding, Da. It's like a stone in my gut."

"Are y'a witch, now, Calum, with the second sight to see the future?" His mockery is sharp, but well meant. "There's no blood of Niall in your veins, son. It's the storm, is all, making you restless. Come sit by the fire with me and have a glass, aye? You'll do no one any good wearing yourself out with the pacing, not to mention the poor floor. You've worn a path in the planks by now."

Calum sighs. "How I can sit and fill my belly with drink when my wife is out there, lost in the storm?"

"She's not lost, Calum, you daft fool. She's on a sturdy, well-built ship captained by a competent man with a lifetime of experience at sea. You helped build the be-damned ship yourself, and you've known Cap'n Patrick your entire life." Da grabs Calum by the arm and physically hauls him out of his bedroom and sits him in an armchair by the fire, then pours a dram. "Stop worrying."

Calum takes a drink, then another. A third. But the whisky settles in his gut like acid, and he sets it aside with a growl. "I know, Da, but . . . I can't shake the feeling."

"This isn't like you, son." Da's craggy features wrinkle with worry. "You're no more a superstitious man than I, to be putting stock in ill feelings."

"Exactly."

"She'll *be* here."

Calum stands, shuffles to find his balance on the thick, gnarled wooden peg that functions as his left leg from the knee down. "I'm going to go down to the docks. I have to do *something*, Da."

Da catches at the gray cable-knit sleeve of Calum's sweater. "It's pissing out, and its past midnight. There's nothing to see and nothing to do but wait. I know it's hard, but its all there is."

Calum shrugs into a slicker, tugs the hood over his head. "I have to go." He pulls a folded square of paper from his pocket, the last letter he got from her, two months ago, holds it up for Da to see.

Da sighs heavily. "Calum, what will you do?"

"Whatever I can do. Anything. Everything." He stomps toward the door, a heavy boot step, and a thunk of his peg. "I have to do *something*."

"You're a one-legged shipwright, and you nearly puked yourself to death on the voyage over." Da's voice is hard, snapping out. "There's nothing you can do, Calum. Sit, and wait."

Calum wrenches the door open, admitting a howl of wind and a spray of rain, and stomps out into the gale. Despite the slicker, he's soaked to the bone within steps, and gives up trying to keep the hood tugged over his head. He peers into the darkness, guiding himself to the docks. There's nothing to see but the occasional glimpse of jagged-edge waves lit by flashes of lightning. The rain drives in sideways sheets, twisted and blown by the wind, each droplet a stinging pellet hammering at Calum's face and pattering relentlessly off his slicker.

His heart is beating out of his chest, thudding wildly. Every instinct he has is screaming at him, telling him something is wrong, something is wrong, something is wrong.

But what can he do?

Nothing.

He's a one-legged shipwright and hasn't stepped foot on a deck sine he lost his leg. There's no captain willing to brave a journey now, anyway, not in this damned monster of a storm.

But she's out there, his sweet, precious wife. "Mary," he whispers, "come back to me."

He clings to a post as the wind attempts to fling him

off the dock and into the bay.

He whispers a prayer to Mary, to Jesus, to every saint he can think of.

His teeth chatter as his blood turns to ice, but he remains on the dock, waiting, praying, and hoping.

At some point, he slips down to sit on the slick wooden planks, both arms wrapped around the dock post. "Come back, Mary," he whispers, again and again. "Come back to me, my love."

At last, with the storm finally beginning to blow itself out, his eyes close and he nods off.

When he wakes, the bay is fogged over, a thick pall of fog the color of sun-bleached bones obscuring everything, even the end of the dock, ten feet away, cannot be seen. He's chilled to the bone, and a tight, thick fist has his lungs in its grip. He struggles to sit up, and a cough wracks him.

"Mary." He wrestles himself upright, every bone aching, every muscle screaming, cough after hacking cough doubling him over.

Between coughs, he hears a telltale sound, the chuck of water against the side of boat. The air is utterly and completely still, as only it can be after a storm like the one that just blew out. Straining his ears, he listens.

There's a creak of shifting wood.

The rattle of a spar clattering against a mast.

"Hello?" Calum shouts. "Hello!"

Silence.

"Mary!" Softer, with a sob: "Mary."

The chucking and the creaking and the rattling continues, growing louder.

And then a tall, fat shape appears out of the fog. A ship. Listing heavily to port. Sail in tatters. Mast snapped off, mainsail gone. The deck is in ruin, and there is not a single sign of life.

The ship drifts slowly, as if set on course by an invisible hand, shoved from the open ocean toward the bay. It doesn't slow as it scuds toward the dock, and shore. Calum realizes it isn't going to stop, and he dances backward awkwardly as the wall of the ship's side crunches into the dock, splintering planks, and grinds to a stop. It shifts further as it settles, listing harder.

The silence is complete.

"Mary?"

The name of the ship—*HMS Victoria*—is blazoned with white paint on the side. This is Mary's ship.

"No. No." He hobbles toward the ship, catches up against the slick wood of its belly.

A line dangles off the side and he snags it, tugs to test it, and then knots the line to the dock. The tide is high and, using the taut line, he is able to haul himself hand over hand up the side of the ship, his one good foot scrabbling at the side, his peg scratching and thumping.

With great effort, he heaves himself over the side, gasping, sweating, slamming onto the deck. He catches his breath, and then lunges to his feet. The top of the mast snapped off and crashed down into the deck, spearing through the planks to reveal the hold below. Peering into the gaping wound, Calum can see crates, bolts of cloth, barrels of foodstuffs, a boot, a dress, all bobbing in the dark water filling the hold.

Calum limps toward the nearest door, leading to the captain's quarters. The room is vacant, books upside-down on the floor, a jar of ink smashed, pens scattered, the window shattered. The guest quarters on the opposite end of the ship are the same, the violence of the storm wreaked its havoc here, too.

"Mary!" He shouts her name, again and again, feeling in his gut the truth.

He slides on his buttocks down the ladder leading into the hold, until he's calf-deep in water. A crate bumps against his knee, and a barrel of tobacco bobs past. A bolt of calico half-unrolled catches against his thigh. Hardtack and biscuits in a broken crate.

A corpse rolls to the surface, twisting and bobbing, bloated. Male, old—the cook. Fish have eaten his face, and Calum's stomach twists.

"Mary!"

In the scant minutes of his presence in the hold, the water level has risen from mid-calf to past his knee—the ship is sinking.

"No . . . Mary . . . Mary." He scrambles back up the ladder onto the deck, and has to haul himself onto the dock from the deck, climbing upward as the ship sinks around him.

He stands on the dock, watching, as the *Victoria* sinks.

Da appears out of the early morning mist and tries to pull Calum away. "It's over, son. She's gone. I'm sorry. I'm so sorry, son, but it's over, it's done."

"No, no. No. Mary. I have to find Mary."

Da gestures angrily at the bit of mast poking up out of the water of the bay. "You found her, son. She's there."

"No!" Calum slams a fist into Da's chest, knocking him backward. "She's not. You don't understand, Da!"

Down the quay, at another dock, a grizzled old man readies his small fishing boat. Calum spies the old man and the tiny boat, and hobbles with determination toward him. He reaches the dock, and grabs at the side of the fishing sloop.

"Are you going out?" he asks.

The old man nods. "Best fishing, just after a storm."

"Take me with you." Calum gestures at the *Victoria*. "My wife was on that ship, and I—I have to find her. Please, help me. Take me out."

"The sea has her, lad. You won't find her."

"I have to try."

A hard, rheumy stare. "You'll sit where I say to sit, and you won't touch nothin'. My ship, my rules."

"Fine, agreed, thank you!" Calum straddles the side of the ship and slides down onto the deck, hopping and hobbling to the crate indicated by the old fisherman.

Da watches, hands in his graying hair, as the sloop vanishes into the fog.

A wind has picked up, shifting the fog into skirling eddies, and it is this wind that blows the sloop out of the bay. The fisherman guides his ship with the easy familiarity of a lifetime's knowledge of the bay and the surrounding area. He listens, head cocked, and then when the clap of the gentle waves echo off the docks and the quay, and the warehouses fades and become a louder kind of silence, he unfurls the sail all the way, unhurriedly tying off lines until the sail bellies to catch the wind.

Calum sits on the crate, staring out into the fog and the waves.

"She was coming from the east," the fisherman rasps. "So it's east we're heading. She'll have left a trail behind her. Corpses and the like."

"How did she make it into the bay? The sail was ruined and the air was still."

"Happens, sometimes." A shrug. "Chance, perhaps. Some say the mer-folk will sometimes return a ship to shore like that, give her a push."

"Mer-folk?"

Another shrug. "Call it superstition if you like, believe it or don't, I care little enough. I've seen 'em."

"Mermaids?"

A nod. "Got blown out to sea, once, many years back, got all twisted around and lost, thought I was sailing for shore but was heading out to sea. Spent days out there, ran out of food and water, thought it was the end. Wind died, becalming me." A long pause, eyes roving the waves. "Saw a face in the brine. A woman. Swam right up and stared at me. Seaweed in her hair, fish scales where her legs should have been. Barnacles growing on her skin. Teeth like knives and hungry eyes. Not a lovely thing, but a fearsome one. I had a full net from my catch aboard, so I tossed the whole rotting mess of fish overboard, and there was a big commotion under the surface. Guts and scales and fish eyes floated up to the surface and, soon enough, I felt my ship moving, being pushed, pulled, I don't know. When we reached the surfbreak they let me drift back in, just like the *Victoria* did." A hard glare, daring Calum to laugh. "That's the damned truth, like it or not."

Calum shivers. "I believe you."

"Don't matter if you do. True is true, whether anyone believes or not." He gestures at the waves. "If your woman is out there, the sea has her. The mer-folk have her. Won't be nothin' to find but sorrow, lad. You'll see."

"Then why are you taking me out?"

"When a man's lost his woman, he's lost his way. You want her to be out there, alive. She ain't, and you know it, but you're just mad enough to believe your own lies. I'll show you the trail of the dead, and maybe you'll find your senses. Or, you'll bury yourself in the waves with your poor wife."

Calum doesn't know what to make of this. "Bury

myself in the waves?"

"You're grief-mad. It's a better end to drown quickly out here, than slowly back ashore." The old man thumps his chest. "Lost my wife in similar circumstances, years ago. Been drowning ever since, but I can't bring myself to let the sea take me. Too stubborn, I guess. I'm doing you a favor. If you want to live, you'll live. If you don't, well . . . like I said, maybe it's better to end it quickly."

Calum's stomach drops out. End it quickly? The thought hadn't occurred to him. He just wants to find Mary, just wants to know she's alive.

But if she isn't?

The thought of seeing her corpse in the waves . . . eaten by fish, bloated . . . Calum loses what little is left in his stomach. If Mary is . . .

He can't even think the word. He's been clinging to the hope that she's still alive.

If she's not . . . Calum tries to imagine carrying on with his life back ashore. Building ships, going to the tavern, drinking whisky with Da . . . it all seems futile and empty and pointless without Mary. How could he continue living? What's the point? Until now, Calum has been clutching desperately at the notion that Mary is out here, alive still, somehow.

If she isn't?

If she's . . . dead?

The idea of sinking peacefully beneath the waves doesn't sound so bad. Better than going through life back ashore without Mary.

"She could still be alive," he insists.

"The sea is full of mischief and trickery and surprises, lad." The fisherman adjusts a line, knots it again. "Never know what's possible, I suppose."

A long silence, and then the fisherman leans far over the side of the sloop and scoops something out of the water—a woman's bonnet. From the bottom of the boat, the fisherman lifts a long pole with a hook on the end and uses it to reach out into the water and pull something toward the boat; the hook is snagged onto the sleeve of a man's coat. The corpse is facedown, but has clearly been in the water a day or two. Now that he's looking, Calum becomes aware of what it is they're sailing through: the wreckage and detritus swept off the deck of the *Victoria*. Another body, also male. Crates and barrels, chunks of broken wood, a bit of spar, clothing. Food. Another body.

Calum cries out, then—this body, the one twisting and bobbing in the waves, is a woman's body. Her dress is splayed out in the water, bits of white petticoat showing. Dark hair floating like a spray of ink.

"Mary!" He leans over the side, reaching for her.

"Stay in the boat, lad," the fisherman warns. "This ain't the spot to be throwing yourself over. You won't find the death you're looking for. Not here."

Calum ignores the fisherman. The woman's body is just within reach, but he can't stretch far enough, can't quite reach . . .

His balance shifts, a wave sends the boat lurching, and Calum is weightless for a moment. Only for a moment, though. He smashes into the icy water, brine salting his lips and stinging his eyes and filling his mouth and lungs. Currents pull at him, and he kicks, thrashes. The sea is dark, so dark, here under the waves.

The woman's body is just beside him, above him.

Her face isn't Mary's.

It's not Mary.

Calum tries to swim, but his coat drags him down, and his peg leg is heavy, and his limbs are tired, and his lungs scream and the current is too strong, pulling him down, down, down.

Something tugs at his foot.

Brushes his shoulder.

He kicks at the current, but the sea has him.

He wants to scream, and the only word jangling through his brain is *Mary, Mary, Mary*, but he can't scream, because his breath is running out.

Something tugs at his knee.

Bumps his back.

Tangles in his hair.

He twists in the current, catches a glimpse of movement in the shadows of the deep. The surface is far overhead. Too far.

Mary.

Mary.

He's dizzy, and his lungs are on fire, and even his desperation is running out. He could take a breath, and it would be over. Why fight any more? The old fisherman was right—the sea has Mary, and now the sea has him.

He kicks for the surface once more, but the current is stronger, pulling him down.

Something colder than the water traces across his cheek, and something tickles his hand. Scrapes his chest. He blinks, salt stinging his eyes, shadows skirling and eddying, darkness deeper than midnight shadows are all around him, pressure crushing him.

Is . . .

Is that a face, there in the shadows? A pale slip of white flesh, just out of reach? A corpse, probably.

But no, it moves. Shifts, too quickly to be caught in the current.

So dizzy.

Fire in his chest.

Darkness in his mind, in his eyes, behind his eyes. Breath is gone, and he has to expel it. His lungs cannot remain contracted any longer.

He's twisted, suddenly. Pulled, pushed.

A face, in front of him.

A woman.

Alive.

Eyes wide and oval, dark, blinking weirdly, inhuman pupils, irises too dark to be human. Too sharp cheekbones. Too high a forehead. Hair too long, too tangled, a wrong shade of brown, almost green, the shade of sea-weed that sometimes washes ashore after a storm. She regards him steadily. Her expression, if a face like hers can be understood to express emotions he would comprehend, is that of someone watching a bug struggling to right itself.

Calum sees her and is sure he must be hallucinating as his lungs give out.

But then she reaches for him, and her palm touches his cheek, and her touch is colder than ice, and far too real. He catches at her wrists, and feels her bones in his hand, her cold flesh.

Calum coughs, then, and knows the end has come. Seawater fills his mouth.

He is sinking.

Drowning.

The woman watches, impassive.

Mary.

Mary?

Does she see the sorrow in him then, this woman of the sea? Does she see something she understands? She moves, a sinuous flicker, and she's catching at him, strong fists clutching at his clothing. Tangling with him, her solid body against his, movement fluttering against his legs.

Her mouth is strange, pressed against his. Alien. Cold, so cold. But her lips feel like lips, and the breath she expels into his mouth tastes of brine and the deepest depths of the sea and other darker flavors, but it is a breath nonetheless, and it fills his lungs and gives him a reprieve from the darkness consuming him from within.

Upward.

She's pulling him upward, swimming for the surface faster than belief. His head breaks the surface, and he gasps for air, coughing, vomiting seawater. The surface of the sea is empty, only waves in every direction. The sloop is gone, the fisherman is gone. There are no corpses, no crates, no barrels.

Calum coughs, kicking to stay afloat, but he's too heavy, too weak, and he sinks beneath the surface, blinking brine, gasping for another lungful of air.

And there she is.

Her bare flesh isn't quite white; is there a greenish tinge? A hint of the jade of the sea, coloring her flesh? She flashes past him, swimming around him.

Calum was a sailor once, before he lost his leg, before he met Mary. He knows the creatures of the sea, the shark, the dolphin, the swordfish, the whale . . .

Her tail is a shark's tail, the fin running vertical, and when she swims, her tail flashes side to side.

Her breasts are bare, and heavy, and round, and now he notices this. Her spine is knobbed, almost ridged. Her shoulder blades are too prominent. There are slits in her skin, at the sides of her throat, which pulse open and closed—gills.

She twists, arching her spine and rolling over, and

then a wicked flash of her tail sends her slicing through the sea toward him, and she's there, up against him, catching at his waist. Her eyes cut over him and see his legs, one whole and complete, and the other ending at the knee, with a gnarled, twisted, polished length of wood where his calf should be.

She tangles a fist in his hair and presses her mouth to his, and once again her breath fills him, tasting stale somehow and briny and of old fish and new meat. He sucks at this breath greedily, out of instinct. His soul is heavy, his heart a vacant hole in his chest, his mind reeling and baffled and overwhelmed, but his body is betraying him, sucking at each lungful of breath he can get, clinging to each next moment of life.

A thousand questions sear through him, tangled and confused.

She wraps an arm around him, and she is so strong, too strong. She pulls him to the surface. She's holding him with one arm, her tail wiggling under the surface, keeping them both afloat. She clings to him, his back pressed to her front, her breasts flattened against his shoulder blades, her hands clutching at his middle. Her tail doesn't merely flick, but beats with staggering power, and they slice through the water together with unbelievable speed.

He can feel the movement of her tail, feel it writhing against his legs, back and forth, back and forth. Her hair streams behind her, like a skein of seaweed. His lungful of air is soon depleted, and he holds it in still, fighting the urge to breathe, to let go.

She angles upward, and rolls to her back with his weight resting on her, and he feels the air on his face and sucks in a breath, and no sooner he has done this than she is twisting once more, powering them beneath the waves.

Again and again, she brings him to the surface, lets him take a breath, and then continues onward. Minutes, hours? He doesn't know, can't track the passage of time except in terms of breaths, lungfuls sucked in and burned through.

The next time she surfaces, there is the sound of waves crashing against shore. Spray flings skyward as the surf smashes against a rock. It is into this violent, white-churned froth of currents and smashing waves that she takes him, to a slick bump of rock. She deposits him onto the rock, and then catches at it with her hands and pulls herself onto it beside him.

"Can you breathe, out of the water?" he asks.

"For a small time." The slits in her throat, the gills, he supposes they are, are opening-closing faster than ever, pulsing rapidly, and he realizes she is winded, exhausted.

"Why does the sea not want me?"

A shrug of her shoulder. "The sea keeps her secrets. I only know she does not want you."

"Mary." Calum points back the way they came. "She was on that boat. With those dead people, where you found me."

A shrug. "The sea keeps her secrets."

"Were you there, when they went overboard?"

Her eyes meet his, and her gaze is alien, utterly foreign. "What is a Mary?"

Calum touches his fist to his heart. "My wife. My mate."

"Oh."

"Did . . . can you find her? My Mary?"

"I know not of your Mary."

The surf is violent, crashing, smashing, deafening, white frothing spray dappling the air: an angry sea.

"I have to know. I have to find her."

"The sea keeps her secrets."

"Then ask the sea! Or show me how to ask!" It's craziness, madness, what he's saying, but Mary was his saving grace, his all, his everything.

She does not answer, which is as much an answer as he'll get.

A few moments of silence between them, leavened only by the crashing surf.

"Are there others like you?" he asks, eventually.

"Are there others like *you*?" she parrots, but it's not a repetition, rather the question returned, the question answered.

She scoops a handful of the surf and splashes herself with it, wetting her face, her throat, her gills, and her lungs expand briefly, her gills pulsing.

"How do you speak my language?" he asks, rather than answering her question out loud.

"Men have known we swim beneath the waves. A man was in the little boat, the little boat that comes out of the larger boat. He was far from any after-sea, lost in the sea. She wanted him and was waiting until it was his time. I tried to help him, but the sea kept him, her currents kept him. So I stayed with him, and learned his words. You men interest me. I like to speak to you. To see you. Your legs are strange."

"How do I find Mary?"

"If the sea has taken her, you cannot."

"I have to find her. I have to find Mary." He meets her eyes, pleading. "The sea can have me, if I can find Mary. She's . . . I have to find Mary."

A shake of her head. "I can help you forget Mary. The sea has her, and the sea does not give up her secrets." She slides across the rock, shimmying closer to Calum. "I can take you down into the waves, and I can help you forget."

"I can't forget."

She touches his wooden leg then the flesh of his thigh above it. "I watch the after-sea, sometimes. From the waves. I watch men and women like me. You mate, like we do."

Calum just stares at her. Seeing her differently. Seeing her as a female. Where her legs would be, where human becomes sea creature, there is a dappling, shadows, rippling, folds, secret flesh, feminine flesh. Breasts. Hands. Lips. Curves and softness where a woman is curved and soft.

She shifts closer to him. Are they closer to the waves, now? Is the surf churning higher around him? Are the waves closer to reclaiming him? He smells her, feels her. She touches him, his legs, his stomach . . . his mind is spinning, dizzy, and a sense of strangeness is flowering in his mind, an otherness, a part of his deepest instincts responding to something in her voice, in the gleam of her eye, in the searing coldness of her touch.

"I watch your men mating with your women. And I think to myself, what would it be like, to mate with a man? To join as we join, but on the after-sea, rather than—"

"But . . . Mary . . ." It's Calum's only coherent thought.

He feels her, this mer-woman, her hands on him, the cold sea air on his bare flesh, her touch so cold it burns, her breath, her too sharp teeth nipping sharply here and there, teasing rather than tearing, her body is familiar and alien at once, her lips firm and her tongue slithery, her breasts heavy and pliable and weighted perfectly in his hands, her flesh like ice, colder than ice, a cold so fierce it becomes fire.

"So warm. Your warmth is strange."

"Cold."

He's not Calum any longer, just a man. Response,

reaction. Her touch leeches his warmth, but her touch also incites heat and need.

"Mary."

He hears a hiss, her sound of frustration. "The sea has your Mary."

"The sea . . ." He's trying to wade through the fog, the haze, the dizziness, the darkness, the strangely urgent desire, trying to remember what was so important. "Then give me the sea."

"I can give you the sea," she says, in a shuddering vibrato that sings in the darkest nooks of his mind. "I can give you the deeps, where there are a thousand Marys to find. The sea can give you the breath of the deeps."

"Only one Mary. *My* Mary." He has her face in his mind, her delicate black strands of hair, the vivid blue of her eyes, the gentle curve of her hips, the slightness of her tender breasts, the quiet murmur of her voice, the strength of her peace, the peace she always gave him so freely, so easily, his Mary was his peace, all she had to do was simply *be*, simply sit beside him and hold his hand and read to him, and he could find his peace in her.

My Mary.

That vibrato sings inside him again. Her touch is so cold, at his temples now, over his heart. The cold filters through him, crackles like ice in his veins. She is all around him, the cold of the depths in her touch, on her lips grazing his skin.

She is inside him, in his dreams, in his memories. The

breath from her lungs pulses through him, he's breathing her breath and the sea is around him, but he isn't cold and doesn't need to breathe the sky, he's breathing her, breathing the sea, she's around him and her touch is warmth.

But still, Mary is all there is. The beat of his heart—*Mary . . . Mary . . . Mary . . . Mary*. He aches, his bones ache, his groin aches. His cock throbs and his balls ache. His heart is fit to burst, pounding in his chest.

Mary.

A day of white: white flowers and white silk, his Navy uniform pressed and creased and pinned at the knee, no veil for Mary, just white flowers in her black hair and the sea behind them, rippling silver and green and blue in the sun. A day of promises, her promise to always be his peace, and his promise to always be her strength, her protector, to shield her from the ugliness of the world, so she can be his innocence, his peace, his whiteness in a blood-red world.

MaryMaryMaryaryMaryMaryMaryMary

The sea whispers around him:

. . . Calum? . . .

Dreams, darkness, memory, death, life—it's all a weirding, twisting tangle. The white of her dress, her lips on his as they kiss for the first time, the white of her skin in the gentle yellow-orange of the firelight, in their cabin by the sea, near the shipyards where he builds ships he'll never set foot on again—it's not seasickness that makes him ill on a ship, but the blood-sickness of memory. The white of her teeth as she laughs at him, teasing, loving. The white of her breasts as she moves above him in the candlelight, such slight, small breasts, so lovely, so pale and delicate and perfect. The white of her thighs around his waist.

White.

Blue, darkness, shadows, purple-black around him. Depths around him like a vise. Hands, teeth, hair that isn't black as raven's wings, as ink, but dark and almost green like seaweed on a storm-wet shore, skin that isn't white, but tinged palest jade, the jade of deepest ocean. Breath that isn't sweet from tea with milk, but sour and salty from devouring strange things scuttling in the sea-deep shadows.

. . . Calum? . . .

Calum. He is Calum.

Mary.

Mary?

He's twisting in darkness, filled with brine-sour shadows. Wrapped up in seaweed and strong arms, lit by some strange unearthly blue-green glow.

He tastes her, the woman from the sea, the mer-woman. Tastes her breath in his mouth, on his lips, feels it in his lungs.

Mary.

There's a hiss. Serpentine, almost. Frustration, anger.

I can give you the sea. She will take you, now. No more longing. No more Mary. No more sorrow.

No, no.

Mary.

Where there is your Mary, there are dreams of your wars, memories of dying in the belly of your ship. I cannot breathe for you a third time. The sea wants you; I am the sea, and I want you.

Mary.

He's drowning in shadows. There is no memory, no susurrus of the past across his mind, only shadows.

Their darkness is broken, incomplete, however. In the shadows, flitting and swimming and seeking, is a flash of white.

White skin

Pale, slight breasts

Ink black hair darker than shadows

A soul that billows lightness and white and warmth

Movement, in the depths.

Warmer sea.

Lighter shadows.

Grayer, rather than fullest black.

One Mary. *My Mary.*

He fights the darkness. Remembers his promise, on the day of white, the day of vows. Love, protect, honor

. . . and always, always, always be her Calum, only her Calum.

Fight the darkness.

Be her Calum.

He can almost hear her, in the twisting currents of the deeps.

. . . *Calum?*. . .

Another hiss of anger.

Movement, a tail beating in the currents, flicking powerfully, driving upward. Currents against his face. Cold, once again.

Sounds: gulls crying raucously in keening shrill overlapping shrieks, the surf on a shore, a bell jangling as a mast dips side to side in the waves. A seal barking.

Sensation: sand skritching under him, water flowing over him, sucking down past him, coldness deep inside him.

Calum coughs, and blinks brine from his eyes. The sky above him is heavy gray, wind blows, rain patters and prattles in a gentle drizzle. He's on a shore, half in the water.

He's not alone.

"You owe me two deaths, Calum." Her voice is a shuddering vibrato, that quavering song in his head, in his soul, a voice that tolls with the power of the tides.

"I only want Mary. I'm her Calum."

She's there, in the sand beside him. Skin and hair tinged green, gills at her throat pulsing. Her teeth are a little too sharp, and a little too many. "I gave you my breath, twice. And now I'm returning you from the sea. The sea wants you, Calum."

The sea wants you; I am the sea, and I want you— he remembers the sound of those words echoing inside him, shuddering in the bone of his skull and the cage of his ribs.

"The sea can have me, but give me Mary."

She glances past Calum, at something down the shore.

A shape. A body, thin and frail and feminine, crumpled in the sand, half in the sea just like Calum.

"Your Mary." That awful, powerful, unearthly vibrato again.

He claws through the sucking surf, his peg digging in the sand, grit under his nails, brine on his lips. He is still caught in the sea, and her currents are sucking him back in.

"No! Mary . . . Mary!" His hoarse rasp grates in his throat. "Mary . . . please, Mary."

She's coughing, belching and vomiting seawater. Rising up on shaky hands, ink black hair stringy and dripping. Her dress is torn, showing her white skin in places.

"MARY!" He claws at the sand and the surf, screaming.

She hears him, sees him, struggles like he struggles,

but the sea has them, and refuses to release them.

"Please!" Mary's voice is as he remembers, quiet, but cutting through noise with its gentility. "Calum . . . please, give me Calum back."

The sea refuses to release them.

Beside him, the mer-woman watches, that impassive, alien expression on her face. "Two deaths. Two lives."

Calum ceases his struggles and twists to regard her. "What? What do you mean?"

"It is the way of the sea. A life for a life. To receive, you must give."

"Give what?"

She glances at his foot, his flesh-and-bone foot, now bare, his boot lost at some point: seaweed is tangled around his ankle, twisted and coiled like a tendril, like a tentacle.

"Your life." She glances at Mary. "Her life."

"What? What do you mean, our lives?"

"When the after-sea has finished with you, you will be called back to us. When the after-sea gives you up, when you feel the breath of your sky fleeing your lungs, you will return to us."

The tendril of seaweed coils around Calum, snaking up his body as if alive, growing around him. Around his wrist. His ankle. His throat. Loops of seaweed, tangled and coiled around him. Squeezing.

"A life for a life, a life for a life." She gestures at Mary, and Calum sees that another tendril of seaweed is snaking around her body as well: throat, ankle, and wrist.

"We have to return to the sea before we die?" He glances at Mary, desperate to go to her, and then at the mer-woman, the creature of the sea.

"Yes." She fingers the seaweed. "This will be your reminder, all of your days walking upon the after-sea."

"But we'll have each other? The sea will give us back to each other?"

"Until you return to her, yes."

"Why?"

A shrug. "Even the sea cannot unknot the strands of fate, Calum." She glances at Mary and then at Calum. "Some loves are fated, and cannot be broken, even by death, even by the sea."

"Anything. As long as I have Mary. She's all that matters."

"She must agree, as well."

"God, Calum—*Calum*." Her voice shakes in his ear.

"Mary! I'm here, Mary. I've got you."

"You borrow the breath of the sky. You borrow your years on the after-sea," the mer-woman says, in that quavering vibrato, the shuddering voice that rolls and tolls in the secret places of their souls.

The seaweed tightens around Calum's throat, around his ankle and wrists, and he hears Mary choking as well, and the sucking grabbing currents pulls them away from shore, back into the hungry brine.

Their eyes meet, Calum's and Mary's, and their hands tangle, fingers twining.

"Yes," Calum gasps.

"Yes," Mary hisses.

The strangling pressure fades, and the currents weaken.

A long moment of silence then, except for the slap of the surf and the cry of the gulls.

Somehow Calum and Mary are tangled together in the sucking surf, currents pulling at their ankles and thighs, and her lips are on his, cold but swiftly warming, and her hands are on his, and her hands do not burn with the coldness of the deep.

"Calum?" Mary's voice, quiet, shaky, tentative.

He rolls toward her, levers himself onto his elbow, and she's there, in his arms, he's breathing her warmth and her pale skin is real, and her whimpering cries are real, and the salt on his cheeks is from tears rather than brine.

"Oh, Mary, Mary." He looks her over, touches her everywhere. "You're real. You're real!"

She clings to his neck. "I think I died, Calum. I drowned." She shivers. "But I heard you. I . . . I saw you, I felt you. You were fighting. A woman . . . that woman . . . *thing*, she had you all wrapped up in her arms and she was going to . . . I don't know."

"You sank, your ship sank," Calum says, "and I thought . . ."

She kisses him, clings to him. "Was it a dream, Calum?"

He feels the seaweed still and pulls away from Mary. Lifts his wrist, showing a thin strand wrapped tight around his wrist and another around Mary's. "I don't think it was."

She shakes and clings to him once more. "You went to sea for me, Calum? You . . . you went back out, went down beneath the waves? After everything you've been through?"

"You were out there, Mary. I had to find you. I'm your Calum."

Mary clings to him fiercely, kissing him everywhere. "We'll go down to the sea together, then. When that day comes, we'll go down together."

He kisses her back, and then, for a moment, he feels an echo of icy skin, a touch so cold his flesh burns, tastes brine-sour breath, and he shudders, pulls away, staring down at Mary to make sure she's real.

"What is it, Calum?"

"She . . . she tried to . . . she wanted me." He shakes his head, unwilling to put to words the dark, twisted images in his mind. "Erase it from me, Mary."

She brushes a stray lock of his damp red hair away from his eye. "How, Calum?"

But her eyes, so blue, so loving, they tell him she knows exactly how.

They crawl out of the surf, away from the reaching

tide, and Mary erases that icy touch with her own, with her warmth, her peace. In the sand, beneath the sky, with the gulls crying and the sea churning, they move together.

Perhaps someone watches from the waves.

Calum doesn't care. His Mary is wrapped up in his arms, the sun warming their bare skin.

Let her watch; their years on the after-sea will be long and full of love. And, after all, as she said . . . some loves are fated, and cannot be broken, even by death, even by the sea.

Some loves are fated, and cannot be broken, even by death . . .

Even by the sea.

Even by the sea.

He sets the pen down, closes the notebook.

His eyelids slide closed, and his breath hitches in his lungs.

"Ava?"

He sees her now, in his mind's eye. Slender, with small, pale breasts. Ink black hair. Vivid blue eyes.

"Ava."

He whispers her name, as if saying her name can summon her, like an ifrit or djinn.

He doesn't remember anything but her face, her name, her body.

Perhaps he can summon more of her, by telling another story.

He opens the notebook and begins to write again. He thinks of her, of Ava. Those blue eyes, that pale skin, her ink black hair, the way she loved him, the way he loved her.

And so he writes, to remember.

TO BE CONTINUED . . .

Visit me at my website: **www.jasindawilder.com**
Email me: **jasindawilder@gmail.com**

If you enjoyed this book, you can help others enjoy it as well by recommending it to friends and family, or by mentioning it in reading and discussion groups and online forums. You can also review it on the site from which you purchased it. But, whether you recommend it to anyone else or not, thank you *so much* for taking the time to read my book! Your support means the world to me!

My other titles:

The Preacher's Son:
Unbound
Unleashed
Unbroken

Biker Billionaire:
Wild Ride

Big Girls Do It:
Better (#1), Wetter (#2), Wilder (#3), On Top (#4)
Married (#5)
On Christmas (#5.5)
Pregnant (#6)
Boxed Set

Rock Stars Do It:

Harder

Dirty

Forever

Boxed Set

From the world of *Big Girls* and *Rock Stars*:

Big Love Abroad

Delilah's Diary:

A Sexy Journey

La Vita Sexy

A Sexy Surrender

The Falling Series:

Falling Into You

Falling Into Us

Falling Under

Falling Away

Falling for Colton

The Ever Trilogy:

Forever & Always

After Forever

Saving Forever

The world of *Alpha*:
Alpha
Beta
Omega
Harris: Alpha One Security Book 1
Thresh: Alpha One Security Book 2
Duke: Alpha One Security Book 3
Puck: Alpha One Security Book 4

The world of Stripped:
Stripped
Trashed

The world of *Wounded*:
Wounded
Captured

The Houri Legends:
Jack and Djinn
Djinn and Tonic

The Madame X Series:
Madame X
Exposed
Exiled

The One Series
The Long Way Home

Badd Brothers:

Badd Motherf*cker

Badd Ass

Bass to the Bone

Good Girl Gone Bad

**The Black Room
(With Jade London):**

Door One

Door Two

Door Three

Door Four

Door Five

Door Six

Door Seven

Door Eight

Deleted Door

Standalone titles:

Yours

Non-Fiction titles:

Big Girls Do It Running

Big Girls Do It Stronger

Jack Wilder Titles:

The Missionary

To be informed of new releases and special offers,
sign up for
Jasinda's email newsletter.